ELVAGE

UNDRALAND

MARY E. TWOMEY

MARY E. TWOMEY, LLC

Elvage

Book Four in the Undraland Series

By
Mary E. Twomey

COPYRIGHT

DEDICATION

Sunday,

Take well-calculated risks,
knowing that your mom, brother, and sister
will always have your back.

STARGAZING WITH FOSS

"He's been gone too many days, Alrik," Foss complained, leaning back against the boat's rail. "We should never have sent Jens to Bedra without a chaperone."

"Patience, friend," Alrik answered, his gray beard outlining his tight smile. "I've never known Jens to fail. He wouldn't stand for it. Too stubborn."

I'd bitten my nails too often for them to appear lady-like. I'd lost my twin brother, my parents, Nik, Tor and Henry Mancini. And now Jens was taking his sweet time coming back to us. He was supposed to be gone one night, but that was a week ago. Jens had been sent to secure horses for us to travel on, plus more supplies since a lot of ours were washed overboard when the farlig fisk attacked Foss's ship.

Well, it was my ship, technically. Since Foss had been

declared dead, I inherited all his possessions due to our sham marriage. Foss and I did not agree on much, but we worked together surprisingly well on the boat. He would show me how to fix a leak or clean a part of it, and I pretty much did whatever he asked. While the others lounged and planned, Foss and I worked until we were exhausted at the day's end. I did anything to occupy my mind so it did not dwell on the very real possibility that Jens was next on the list of people I loved that were now six under.

"Not like that," Foss said, correcting the back and forth hand movement I was using to scrub the walls. "You need to go in a circle, or it won't be even. Everyone knows that."

"Sorry. Like this?" I changed my scrubbing accordingly.

"Is it in a circle?" he asked.

"Yup."

"Then that's how I want it."

If I was new to Foss's "cheery" nature, his constant negativity and criticism would have been tiresome. But having grown used to his personality, I did not take offense. I was too concerned with Jens's prolonged disappearance to properly argue with Foss.

This seemed to be the only thing that softened the brute. That, and my brother Charles Mace had done his freaky Huldra whistle a few more times to strip away bits of the curse that kept Foss the surly jerk he was. That had been a long night of Foss puking overboard while I held him. Since his last stripping two nights ago, he was noticeably less argumentative.

"Do you want me to start over? I can do it all again with your circle swipes on the deck." I had maybe three feet left to wash on the entire ship, but it didn't faze me. I wanted the distraction.

Foss examined my work and shook his head. "No. Just remember for next time."

"Okay." I finished up and threw my rag in the bucket. I was sweating from head to toe, but didn't care. It's not like I was gunning for a beauty pageant or anything. My jeans had seen better days, and my purple tank top had dirt and blood stains on it from our various adventures. I stood and stretched my arms over my head, twisting my waist to get some feeling back in my body. "What's next, boss?"

It was rare for me to surprise Foss, but the shirtless hulk of a man looked at me like I'd just started speaking in French. "It's almost dark."

"You can go to sleep, but I'm not tired. What else needs to be done?"

He looked around, casting for things we'd not tackled. "Nothing really. A few things we'll need daylight for. Repairing nets is impossible in the dark."

"I've got good eyes. Show me how," I demanded. The others were eating in the galley, but I had no interest in socializing or eating more of the stale, powdery biscuits. There was a tin of random-meat jerky left, but honestly, I'd rather chew on the dirty rag I'd just cleaned the boat with.

"Everyone else is eating," Foss pointed out.

"Oh. Go ahead. You must be starving." I rubbed the

back of my neck. Though it had been a couple weeks since my long blonde hair had been lopped off to an inch below my chin, it still felt strange to have the wind touch my neck. "Where are the nets? I'm sure I can figure out how to fix them."

"Take a break, little rat." He mussed my filthy hair with something that almost resembled affection. "Rat" used to be strictly derogatory. After we survived Fossegrim together, there was less hatred in his dealings with me.

"Nets?" I asked again. If I stopped, everything would come crashing down on me. The deaths, the fear... and Jens.

To be clear, it wasn't that I missed my boyfriend, which of course, I did. The thing that kept my hands working was the thought that he would never come back, which was a very real possibility.

Foss gave me a hard look, and then led the way to one of the rooms below deck. He yanked out giant rope nets that weighed at least triple one soaking wet me. He hauled them up to the deck so we could take advantage of what was left of the dipping sun. Opening the bundle up on the wood floor, he pointed to a frayed edge. "See that? It needs fixing. And this?" He showed me a severed knot. "Retying would do the trick." He brought up a box filled with supplies I would need. "But it can all wait until tomorrow. I was going to do it anyway. We're running low on food, so I was planning on taking the boat out a little ways to catch some fish."

"You're giving up on Jens coming back," I stated flatly, fingering the edge of the net.

Foss rolled his eyes. "You're so dramatic. The Mare won't kill Jens. They'll just... detain him. He's fine. Taking his sweet time, but fine. I'm not giving up. I'm catching dinner so we can eat while he wastes our time."

"Okay." I nodded, sitting down on the deck and pulling the net onto my lap. "Go on down and eat something."

Foss looked like he wanted to argue, but left anyway. As much as I loved when he was gone, his absence left me alone with my thoughts, and my thoughts these days were pretty grim. I couldn't shake the memory of my rabid dog snapping to get at me from Jens's arms, and the awful sound he made when Jens killed him.

Images of Jens with an arrow through his chest flooded my brain before I could stop them. Jens with a knife in the back. Jens on a guillotine. Jens beaten up and left rotting in a ditch. He was Superman to me. Something about the feel of waiting in angst for your protector to return can make a girl nuts. Nuts enough to clean an entire pirate ship.

I did a thorough job with the nets, going through each little notch, inspecting it for any signs of weakness, and repairing the parts when I saw fit. It was the perfect task – never-ending.

The others ate and turned in for the night. Britta and Jamie hugged me, looking only mildly concerned for Jens's welfare. Jamie treated the whole thing like an annoyance, as if Jens was purposefully being detained. Britta was not as concerned as I thought a sister should be, but I took her gentle strength as a rubric for how freaked out I would allow myself to be on the outside. On the inside, I would go nuts and bolts. To the world, I would quietly tie knots in a fishing net alone in the corner on my dead husband's ship. Totally emotionally balanced.

Alrik gave me a kiss on the top of my head, and Charles hugged me before poking me in the side with his prehensile tail to provoke a tease out of me. He earned a simple smile, which he seemed satisfied with, thank goodness.

With everyone tucked in their hammocks down below, I sat in the red moonlight with the repair kit as I looped and knotted.

"Would you stop it?!" Foss cried from across the deck. I could see his neck muscles tensed even in the light of Undra's giant moon.

I stilled, turning to him. "What?"

"The rocking you do. It's deranged! Just go to bed. You'll send me over the edge if you keep this up."

"What rocking?"

Foss smacked his forehead. "You don't even know you're doing it! You were rocking back and forth like a madwoman. Go to sleep, Lucy. We're docked. There's no reason for you to work like this."

"Am I being loud?" I snapped.

"No. You barely run your mouth anymore."

"Am I in the way over here in the corner, or when I was cleaning the boat with you all day?"

"No."

"Then shut up about it. I'm not hurting anyone. Go to bed. You're starting to get crabby all over again. Don't make me call Mace up here to strip that curse off you again."

Foss stomped back down the stairs, resurfacing minutes later with a biscuit and bit of beef leather. Delish. He shoved the food scraps at me. "Here. Eat."

"Oh. Thanks." I took the food and eyed him with the signature skepticism we regarded each other with. "Why are you being nice?"

"I'm not allowed to be nice?"

"I don't trust it." I sniffed the biscuit for signs of poisoning. He rolled his eyes at my skepticism as he sat down a few feet from me. I took in his less than aggressive demeanor and shifted my attitude accordingly. "Aren't you tired?"

"Exhausted," he admitted, surprising both of us with his honesty. "I'm not looking forward to the trek back to Elvage. Circhos roams the forest. He's more of a pain than you, if you can imagine. I'm not sure how Alrik's planning on getting close enough to the portal to destroy it. Security was pretty heavy when we left."

I thought back on our failed attempt. "I never really worry about the plan when Uncle Rick's on it. I don't really need to see how the rabbit comes out of the hat. I just enjoy the show and clap when I'm told."

Foss gave a companionable snort. "You know, I think I'm around you too much. I actually understood that." He leaned against the side of the boat and folded his hands behind his head. "He's fine, you know."

My fingers slipped on the knot I was retying. "Yup."

"You should get some sleep. Tomorrow I'll teach you how to catch fish with the nets. You'll like it, but you'll need your strength."

I nodded, taking in his big brotherly words curiously. I took a bite of the biscuit and swore off disgusting sand bread as soon as proper food reentered our lives. "Look. This whole you being nice thing is great, but I keep expecting an anvil to fall on my head or something. Why the sudden change?"

Foss did not look at me as he spoke, but cast his eyes up to the stars that were sparkling next to the giant moon I knew I would never get used to. He sighed. "It's my ring around your neck."

I looked down at the heavy gold ring and giant ruby stone with his crest emblazoned on the sides. "Oh. I told you that you could have it back. I don't have to wear it if it bothers you."

"No. Keep it. It's one of the few things I've done that I'm actually a little proud of."

"Huh. I thought you hated me."

Foss grinned, scratching his bare chest. "Oh, make no mistake. I wish you were anyone else."

I pointed to his heart. "That's my darling husband."

"But you were in a tough spot. I'm glad I stepped up and paid Jens back by speaking for you."

"I really hate that term."

"Why do you think I keep using it?" He aimed his smile at me, and I could tell there was a tease behind the mean words. Foss was actually being playful. Huh.

"Well, I appreciate it."

He eyed the ring with a faraway expression. "I swore if I ever did marry, I'd treat my wife like a queen."

I scoffed. "You hate women. You hate me. What makes you think a ring would magically change all that?"

"It's just not how I pictured it. I don't really know what to do with you."

"Nothing. Do nothing with me. I don't need to be handled. You're being fine. Teach me how to work our boat."

"My boat."

"Technically, it's mine, but I'll let you think it's still half yours."

"And we're back to hate," he joked. "You need to sleep."

"I had a dad, and he stopped telling me when to go to sleep at like, seven. I have a boyfriend who treats me like an adult most of the time. Who do you suppose you are that you get to tell me what to do?"

With a solemn face, he answered, "I'm your husband."

I laughed. I couldn't help it. He was just so sincere. My hand tapped my heart to let him know that he touched something tender and cute. "Oh, darling husband, you're in for such a surprise when we get to my world."

"You need to sleep," he repeated, gently taking the net

away from me. "Jens will come back. Punishing yourself like this isn't going to bring him home any sooner."

I had nothing to say to this. He was right, and what was more confusing, he decided to be a decent guy for once. That, coupled with malnutrition and sleeplessness, made for a lapse in my smart retorts. "I, um, I guess you're right." I muscled my way through the rest of my biscuit. "Thanks. You know, you're not a complete tool every now and then."

"Thank you?" he said with half a smirk. He tilted his head back and pointed to the charcoal sky. "Sleeping under the stars again?"

Since he was attempting polite conversation, I decided to take a chance and ride that train. The worst he could do was push me off it. Again. "Yeah. Doesn't feel right sleeping in the hammock without Jens or Henry Mancini."

Foss slid down so he was lying supine on the floor. He jerked his chin to the empty spot next to him. "Come take a break."

I eyed the spot warily, checking it for booby traps before settling down next to him. "You know, Jamie'll feel it if you dump my body overboard. Built-in security detail."

He chuckled and pointed to a cluster of stars overhead. "That's *Orwandil*. It means bad fortune, and it settled right in the middle of the sea. It's usually closer to Bedra." He pulled me closer so our sides were touching. "I should've looked at that before we shoved off. Might have given us a decent warning."

His skin was cool to the touch, so I rubbed his stomach

to warm it, smiling a little when I could tell I'd hit a ticklish spot. "It just looks like a mess of lights to me. How can you tell what's what?"

"Years of practice. That one's my star." He was singling one out in the sky, but I couldn't separate the lights. "Everyone in Undra has a star that tells their story. It moves with them."

"Seriously? Are you just making this up to see how gullible I am? Because I'm pretty tired and would believe almost anything at this point."

He glanced at me as if I was an idiot. "Of course it's true. There I am, right above us." He moved his eyes back up to the heavens. "And if you're tired, you should go to sleep."

"Then why would Olaf believe you're dead? He can just look up and see which star's yours."

Foss cracked a modest smile as he spoke. One of his arms reached over his torso and brushed against my fingers, touching the tips like little kisses as he directed our hands to his navel. "Stars aren't something educated people put a lot of hope in. Most write it all off as myth, but my mother knew better. She taught me how to find people's stars and use them for tracking. I can predict the weather, hunting trends, tide flow – lots of things just by looking up at the stars. It's not always clear, but sometimes the sky speaks to me."

"You're totally serious right now." I was amazed that he indulged in something so poetic. "You know, if we get over to the Other Side, you have to try this out on a girl. It's a pretty good line. Very romantic."

"It's not a line. It's the truth." He motioned up to a tiny star that kept sparking from dull to super bright. "That one's you. I noticed the change in the sky the night you crossed over. See how it flickers? The more violent the swing, the worse your state is. It's how I knew you weren't doing so well tonight."

My mouth dropped open. "Are you serious? That one there? That's me?" My voice quieted, and I could hear the ocean gently lapping at the boat. "I have my very own star?"

"You do. No matter where you go, I can always find you using your star." His other hand wound through my hair, twirling around the curls as if we had no cares in the world at all.

"That's... that's pretty cool, Foss."

"Watch that one there. The bright one to the left."

I rolled onto my side, and snuggled up next to the meanest man I'd ever been forced to work with, marveling at both the star and the oddity of life's wild waves. "It's pretty," I commented. No sooner had the words escaped me did the star blink and shoot across the sky. "Whoa! Did you see that? How did you know it was going to do that?"

"Lots of nights on this boat. I told you. My mother taught me well. I'm the only one of the four powers that started off as a slave. The others dismiss the stars, but it's how I was able to build up my kingdom."

"Hey," I said, changing the subject. "I bought you something when you sent me shopping before we left."

"Did you buy me a real wife?" he teased, picking up my fingers that were tangled through his so he could examine them.

"Ha. No, I bought you a fiddle. I know you don't play anymore, but in case you wanted the option, I wanted you to have it. Went overboard, though."

Foss was quiet for an entire minute before speaking. "I don't play anymore." His words and tone were finite, so I knew not to push him.

I was familiar with the loss of a desire to play. I recall being a lot more fun before Linus died. I took a chance and leaned up, pressing a light kiss to Foss's temple to acknowledge whatever pain he'd gone through to get him to the point in life where play was not an option anymore.

Foss turned his head and pushed his lips to my forehead, holding me there a few beats as he breathed into my skin with his eyes closed. "For what it's worth, you're not the worst wife a man could have."

I don't know why I took his bitter words as a sincere compliment, but I draped my arm around his chest, holding him as strangely as he held me. I didn't understand our dynamic, but I was too tired to run from it anymore that night.

Though my shoulder was uncomfortable on the flat hard surface, my body relaxed at the first promise that I'd decided to stop working it to death. Exhaustion flooded my senses, and I yawned into his neck as Foss told me stories about different adventures he'd had on this very ship. He sounded like a pirate as he talked about searching out different islands for various resources, and which ones had the easiest locals to trade with.

I'm pretty sure I muttered "goodnight" or something to that affect before I succumbed to my body's wailing for a night of rest. Whatever strange twist of fate landed me under the stars lying with my temple pressed to Foss's neck, I decided not to question it. I welcomed the small amounts of peace I could grasp at and fell into a deep sleep as the waves rocked us with their gentle caress.

2

———

PERSONALITY SWINGS

awoke to the sea and the scent of Foss's skin. My eyes flew open, verifying with a note of dread that I had indeed fallen asleep snuggled up to the man who had slapped me across the face and degraded me at every turn. I blamed this poor choice on delirium and vowed to start eating and sleeping regularly to avoid such catastrophes in the future.

He looked younger without his perma-scowl. His lips were parted slightly in sleep, and though we were sworn enemies, I allowed myself to rest in the arms of the dragon for a handful of moments, wishing he was not handsome so he would be easier to resist.

I tried to sneak out of his arm that had fallen across my hips, but the movement woke him.

"What happened?" he mumbled, just as confused as I at our close proximity. When he realized where his hand was, he jerked away from me, sitting up with his familiar glower.

"Ah. There's my darling husband."

"Don't talk to me." He shook his head, trying to get a good grasp on the situation. "It's that halfy. His whistle keeps messing me up." He looked at me out of the corner of his eye, clearly embarrassed. "It's his fault."

"I'll be sure to distrust anyone who can turn you into a halfway decent guy. Shame on Charles for making life with you bearable. You know, I knew it had to be too good to be true. I knew the only way you would be cool is if someone changed your personality on a magical level."

He scowled at me. "I don't know what you're grinning about. There's loads of work to do. Quit lying around and get to it. But wash up first. You're disgusting."

"Whatever. You were totally falling in love with me last night. Bound to happen. I'm awesome, and any other woman would have stabbed you in your precious little sleep by now. Match made in Heaven."

"Ugh. We're getting Jens back today. He can stand being around you."

"That's the spirit!" I cheered, pumping my fist in the air. "When's the search party go out?"

"I've got a fair guess where he is."

My mouth fell open in disgust. "Huh? Why didn't you say something? If he's being held somewhere, why wouldn't you tell us?"

Foss cracked a smarmy smirk that made me want to

smack him. "Because Jens doesn't want to be found right now. He's blowing off some steam, as you call it."

"I've been worried sick about him, and you've been sitting on this intel? You're a bastard!" I stood just so I could tower over him and lecture the jerk-wad. "Let's go get him! Take me there now."

Foss cottoned onto my attempt at intimidation and stood, his massive form swallowing mine. "I'd like to know when you decided it was a good idea for you to give me orders. You're the rat. I'm the master."

"Screw you!" I shouted. I heard the others stirring below and felt slightly bad for waking them only a little after dawn. "Take me to Jens. We've got one more portal to hit before I get to go home." I put my hands on my hips and looked him dead in the eye. "You want to get rid of me? Find Jens. Sooner this is over, the sooner we never have to see each other again."

Foss considered this, and as much as I could tell it pained him to admit my way was the right one, he nodded, shoulders deflating. "Fine. But only so I don't have to share a world with you anymore."

I donned my most patronizing tone and spoke to him in my best preschool teacher voice. "Oh, but how are you gonna get to sleep at night without me to snuggle?"

That did it. Foss raised his hand to strike me, but I dodged, backing away from his flaring PMS.

My voice rose, and I could hear the slice of madness escaping my usually cool demeanor. "You can dish it out, but you just can't take it, huh. Well, joke's on you, Foss, because I got nothing to lose! Nothing! I'm not afraid of you anymore!"

Foss grabbed me by my tank top and yanked me up, raising my feet up off the floor. I matched his snarl with my own. "You need to learn to shut your mouth," he warned, his face inches from mine.

"You need to learn to control your temper!" I challenged.

He carried me to the side of the ship, flipped my legs over the railing and dangled me over the edge by my wrists. "Had enough?" he roared.

"I had enough of you the first time you opened your fat mouth!"

Okay, probably not the smartest thing to provoke the bear while I was at his mercy, but the jolt of him going from loathing me to liking me to snuggling me to hating me all over again was jarring. I wasn't exactly making the best decisions.

"Whoops!" He pretended to drop me, lowering me a few inches. We were the only boat for miles along the white sandy beach, but he still looked around to make sure we did not draw attention.

Jamie bolted up the stairs, having seen the whole mess I'd gotten myself into through our link. "Stop it, Foss! The water's too shallow. You'll break our legs!"

I heard Charles shout for me as he ran toward us. So dramatic. Like I couldn't handle a fight with Foss.

"Do it!" I goaded him. "I could use a good swim. You pick a fight with me? Finish it, coward! Using your big, bad strength instead of your teeny tiny brain? So typical!"

Foss ground his teeth together as he glared down at me, wanting to drop me but knowing he wouldn't get away with it now there was an audience present. In a curl I could not help but be impressed by, Foss lifted me up and dragged me back over the rails, depositing me in Mace's arms.

My brother was more shaken up than I, looking me over and checking my wrists for damage. "I'm fine," I assured him.

His tail wrapped around my hip and pulled me behind him. Charles stared down Foss with anger I'd not seen on him before. "Don't touch her again."

"Keep your Huldra powers out of my head, then!" Foss roared back. "You're trying to change me. Don't!"

Charles brought me to his chest and covered my ears. He pursed his lips and let out a three-noted whistle that brought Foss to his knees. Foss's hands went over his ears, but it was too late. I could tell he was softening.

Watching Foss get the Depravity of Man curse stripped from him was a bit like watching a bull go through an exorcism. He fell to all fours and snorted like a beast, his stomach bouncing inward and out more violently than was natural. It was as if the curse was buried in his belly, which had to be emptied at every stripping.

Jamie and I dragged Foss over to the railing seconds

before he lost his dinner, lunch and anything else still processing in his gut. Vomit rocketed out of him as if it was being punched out of his body. He gripped the railing until the last heave choked him. He collapsed so quickly, Jamie barely caught him before he hit the deck. I kissed Foss's forehead, my anger softening as he whimpered in my arms. Foss's shoulders slumped, and he breathed like he had just run a mile.

Charles geared up for another round, but I simply couldn't take it. I was still sensitive to people barfing in my presence ever since Linus's many failed chemo treatments. I jumped up and placed my hand on Mace's sternum. "Stop, Charles. It's fine. I was pissed, so I poked back this time. He's a child. I shouldn't have engaged. Foss can't take anymore right now."

Mace hugged me and kissed the top of my head. "I don't care how it happened. No one's allowed to throw you overboard except for me. Got it?"

I smirked, despite the situation. "You're throwing me overboard? Says who?"

"Says me. The next time you go angering the hive, I'll throw you in the water to save you from yourself." He kissed my cheek, and this time I actually let myself feel the comfort he was always trying to give me. I missed Linus with all my heart. Every day was twenty-four hours without half of myself. Having a brother again had its benefits.

"Foss knows where Jens is," I told him loud enough for

my voice to carry to Jamie, who was looking over the railing to see if I would have actually broken anything had I been dropped.

Charles rubbed my back. "We all know where Jens is. Why do you think none of us is worried? We would've gone out to look for him days ago if there was any doubt."

"What? Where? Foss said he was probably being held somewhere."

Jamie shook his head at Charles in warning. I knew that look. It was universal guy code for "don't narc on your boy to his girlfriend". I poked at his brain, but Jamie threw up a wall to keep me out. My psychically linked buddy spoke to me in a voice that was too light for normal conversation. "He'll be back when he's ready. I haven't told you about my grandfather, have I? Loads of fun, that one. He could make quality Gar out of anything."

"Save it," I snapped. "Where's Jens?"

"He'll be back," Jamie repeated. When this did not satisfy, he said, "Lucy, it's better if you don't ask too many questions. He's safe. He does this a few times a year when it's been a rough one. He always resurfaces after a week or two."

Charles stared down Jamie. "She's got a right to know. If he's going to be carrying on like this, I don't feel the need to protect him."

Jamie's sarcasm was uncharacteristically thick. "Oh, you'd like that, wouldn't you? Stir things up for Jens so Lucy breaks it off with him."

"Huh?" I whipped my head back and forth between them, now irate. "That's it. I've heard enough. I'm going. Guy vacation or not, he's been gone longer than the two days he promised. I have faith in Jens. If he missed his date, it's because something went south. He wouldn't ditch me like that. Something's wrong, and I'm worried."

Charles rubbed my back again. "I didn't mean to make you upset, *kära*. He'll come back."

I stomped off to the bathroom, ignoring the calls of the guys. I bathed for the first time in two days and changed into fresh jeans and my good old red Partridge Family t-shirt that was beginning to feel like a second skin with how often I wore it. My hair was still damp when I resurfaced in the galley, reluctantly pocketing a piece of beef bark and grabbing a canteen. Jamie, Britta and Alrik were lounging at the table, talking about where was best for Foss to cast his nets.

"I'm going," I stated apropos of nothing. "So Jamie, if you don't want one heck of a headache, get your shirt and shoes on and take me to Jens."

Jamie rested his face in his hands. "Alrik, please tell your niece she can't go see Jens."

A hard look flickered across Uncle Rick's face before he replaced it with his usual grandfatherly affection. "Goosy, dear, what a wonderful idea. I'm tired of waiting for Jens, as well. We've got a job to do, and I think we've had enough respite."

Jamie grumbled into his hands. "That is not what I asked."

Alrik tapped his fingers lightly on the table, calculating my resolve. "I see no need to treat my niece like a child. She killed a Werebear, survived the Nøkkendalig, blew up the farlig and made herself a chief Tribeswoman in Fossegrim. Whatever's detaining Jens, I'm certain she can handle it," then he leveled his gaze at me in silent threat, "with maturity and grace."

Britta did not stand when Jamie reluctantly moved to the exit. He looked over his shoulder at her. "Aren't you coming?"

Britta's laugh was bitter as her head tilted back. "I have no desire to see my brother making a fool of himself. Though I will miss out on the thrashing this one's sure to give him." She gestured to me with an air of sisterhood. "Leave grace here, Lucy. Give him everything you've got. Maybe you can force him to grow up. Heaven knows I never could."

Confusion began to deflate the wind from my sails. I readied a spare sack of supplies, not sure how long the journey would be as I waited for Jamie to get ready. Whatever Jens was up to, I wasn't waiting around like a chump to find out.

3

SEARCHING FOR JENS

"I'm telling you, whatever you think he's been doing, you're wrong." I tromped through the thick green overgrowth that climbed up to my waist. "Jens loves me. He isn't purposefully not back. Something's wrong, Jamie. I just know it."

"Just be prepared for the possibility you might be wrong on this one." Jamie hacked away at a thorny flower vine that impeded our progress. "As someone who's been his best friend for as long as you've been alive? You might want to take my word on this one."

"Jens loves me," I repeated, though this time with less conviction.

Had I known what a gorgeous place Bedra would be, I would have insisted on cutting through there first thing. There were tall palm trees with bright pink mangoes, not coconuts growing from them. The ocean lapped up to white sanded beaches that outlined the mainland. The three-foot tall grass was lush and soft with huge blue flowers poking out so high, they climbed up to my shoulders. There was a cool note in the warm breeze that was so restful; all I needed was a good rendition of *Margaritaville* to complete the picture of perfect peace.

Of course, the pit in my gut was twisting so much, I was unable to really enjoy the bizarre tropical scenery. We had been walking all day, and I didn't get the sense we were actually getting anywhere. "I feel like you're leading us the wrong way," I mumbled as we stepped over a stream I could swear looked familiar.

Jamie gave me a non-response that did not inspire confidence. We walked in silence another hour before he spoke. "We're close to The Den."

"Den of what?" I stopped beside him and took a swig from my canteen.

"The Mare's lair. It's called The Den. It's where people like Jens go to unwind."

"What are we about to walk into?" I asked warily. "What do I need to know about the Mare?"

"Bedra is made of mostly women. They prey on the energy of men who pass by."

"Come again?"

"The most beautiful women in our world are Mare, except for Britta, of course."

"Nice save. I'll be sure she gives you your brownie points."

Jamie smirked and sat on a stump to rest his legs as he geared up to explain the unpleasantness of the world to me. He had that same determined face my parents donned when laying out the birds and the bees. "Mare feed on the wills of men. They buy barrels of the lavender powder from the Fossegrimens to lure men to The Den. They use their... womanly ways and the powder to get the men to sleep. Then they sit on their chests and implant horrific nightmares in them. The men wake up exhausted and disturbed, so they crave more distractions and more lavender powder to make them forget. Night after night, the Mare feed on the wills of the men, and their prey get weaker and weaker. Eventually the men forget themselves completely and live out their days in The Den. Some have been here for years."

I'm sure I gasped, but my mouth had fallen open somewhere around "womanly ways".

"The Mares only have daughters. No sons. So the only men they get are passersby. They don't like to let them go." He wiped a bead of sweat from his brow. "Bedra is great for men who don't believe in the Land of Be. They can't check out in Be, so they check out here."

I was silent, and Jamie waited patiently for my mouth to catch up with my stuttering brain. "Why is Jens here?" I asked, dreading the answer.

"He used to be a regular. Lots of guys like the thrill of the Mare. Unlimited lavender powder and plenty to look at. He's something of a celebrity everywhere he goes, and the Mares work extra hard to keep him sedated. He's a big win for them. Puts up a good fight, so it takes longer to drain the will from him." Jamie refused to look at me. "He used to go there a lot before he started working for your family. Alrik got him that job in part to save him from himself and his devices."

"W-Why? Why did he go there? What was he running from?"

"Well, there's my father, for one. He's tried to kill Jens quite a few times. The trolls did a number on his back, so at first he started taking the powder for medicinal reasons. It's a quick descent into addiction from there. Then there's the overnight fame that spawned from being the bravest warrior in the country. Jens is a private person. He didn't like the chaos that came from being the most desirable bachelor in Tomten." He took a drink from my canteen. "So Alrik found him a job where he could be invisible. He only went to Bedra a few times a year after that. I don't know why he never kicked the habit."

Horrible images flooded my imagination. "What am I going to see in The Den?"

Jamie peeled a leaf from a nearby vine and chewed on it, offering another to me. The flavor was minty mixed with a sort of banana flavor or something sweet. "Hopefully we won't find him here, right? You seemed pretty sure he was being detained somewhere. Maybe you'll get lucky and that'll be true."

"Excellent options," I muttered. I thought over what I

knew of Jens compared to the vast abyss I did not know. My resolve solidified. "I know Jens. We won't find him there."

Jamie gave me that pitying gaze that made me secretly rage every time. "Okay, Lucy."

4

JUST A MAN

*W*hatever I had found Bedra to be thus far, it was not the depravity I found in The Den. I realize I sound like a dowdy old schoolmarm, but legit, the second I walked in I felt the creeping need for hand sanitizer and rubber gloves. The very smell that descended upon me made my nose burn with citrus that felt like it fizzed in my nose, entering my brain and making me slightly lightheaded in a solitary breath. The mud walls were sticky with something that looked and felt like honey, but they stank of musk and vice. I gave those a wide berth.

The woman that greeted us a few feet in had thick black makeup around her eyes. It was the only time I'd seen makeup in Undra, and it was overdone even for a sitcom stereotyped transvestite. She wore a purple sort of loose, thin bra that barely covered her perkiness, and the sheer skirt she wore had seven slits up the sides all the way to her underwear.

I felt vastly overdressed in my jeans and T.

The hostess eyed Jamie with a calculating stare. Without a greeting or his consent, she reached out and touched his hand, stroking the inside of his palm as if checking for something telling. "You've come to collect Jens," she purred in her low, seductive voice. "Prince Jamie, you always spoil our fun."

"Indeed," Jamie answered in an even tone, retracting his hand slowly and wrapping his arm around me. "Though I wouldn't be too sad, Brigit. He always comes back for the lure of Bedra." He looked past her, but the dark muddy hallway did not lead to anywhere we could see. "Jens is here, then?"

The woman did not regard me at all or greet me. In fact, it seemed her eyes passed clear over me. "What if I said no?"

Jamie gave her a polite smile that seemed groomed in a politician's son. "I'm fairly certain you're not allowed to say no to me."

I shivered at his cold words and tried not to shrink at the very adult conversation. Jamie's hand on my back was supposed to bring comfort, but I think I was beyond that at this point.

Brigit leaned forward and kissed Jamie on the lips. A long, drawn out lip lock that screamed sex. I watched in horror as he closed his eyes and indulged her in the few seconds of passion that seemed almost like a rite of passage into The Den. When she pulled away, I gawked at Jamie.

"Right this way," Brigit beckoned, leading the way with her sashaying hips down several halls that slowly sloped down into the earth. I had the distinct impression I was being closed inside when the honeyed mud walls and the stifling citrus only grew stronger and more intrusive as we went.

"Are you surviving?" Jamie asked in a soft voice.

I didn't realize until then that I was holding his hand. "I need a shower." I bristled, scowling at him, recalling my indignation. "And I'm telling Britta you kissed that girl. Bros over hos."

Jamie gave me a questioning look, and then chuckled when my phrasing resonated. "She knows how to get into The Den. I've come here to dig Jens out with her many times. You can't get in without handing over a small amount of your will to the Mares."

"Do *not* leave me in here," I begged as we turned the corner. I squeezed his grip. "This hand doesn't leave yours until we see the light of day again." The lanterns had red gauzy material draped over them, giving the distinct red light district feel. The Police's *Roxanne* starting playing in my head as I tried unsuccessfully to blend.

There were dozens of women lounging everywhere, and maybe seven men. The men sat on plush circular couches in various stages of undress. The women were either all naked or mostly there, doing their seduction in slow motion. I cringed and held tight to Jamie. This was way out of my element.

When I cast around for Jens, I took in the expressions of the men being fawned over. They did not look excited at the plethora of goods to be fondled and ogled. They looked exhausted. Bags under their bloodshot eyes, sallow yellowed skin, and either bloated or sunken in bellies. No one was smiling, yet they were determined not to miss a moment. I got it, but man, was it sad to watch. Reminded me of the typical overindulgence of a man sitting in a dark basement watching too much porn, neglecting daylight and the real world.

There was no way Jens was here. I just knew it.

Brigit led us to a private room and ran her hand up Jamie's thigh as she opened the door. The familiar feeling of wanting to stab someone for being skeezy to a man I loved rose up in me. It was then that I realized Jamie had taken a sort of older brother role in my life. I squeezed his hand again.

The first thing I saw was a bowl of lavender powder, which Jamie steered me away from. The second thing my eyes landed on was Jens. I gasped at the scene before me, wishing for it not to be real. Jens was naked, lying on the mud floor completely unconscious. Two voluptuous women sat on his torso. One had her hand over his mouth and the other had her hand on his forehead. They were focusing hard, and I guessed they were in the process of sucking out bits of his will to feast on. Succubus in action.

The air was already too thick for comfort, but the sight made each breath absolutely unbearable. I don't know how long I stood there, letting the shock bash me over the head like a mallet, but I didn't come to life until Brigit touched the ring on the strap around my neck. She stood too close for comfort, and I really hoped I wouldn't be expected to kiss her. As it was, I could barely feel my legs.

"This is Master Foss's ring," she stated, examining the etching of his crest on the side. She looked at me with new appreciation. "Foss took a wife? I never thought I'd live to see that come to pass."

"Yup. My husband sent me to collect Jens, so if you could wrap things up, he'd appreciate it."

She looked me up and down with a curious eye. "What are you? Too tall and slender to be a dwarf."

My already broken heart ripped open further at the thought of Tor sinking in the abyss.

Brigit ran her hand up my side, and I backed away on instinct. "You're too short to be anything else." She fingered my hair, marveling at the color. "A Guldy. I could've guessed Foss would choose a prize to show off to the other chiefs." The she whispered in my ear, "You're welcome to stay, little *kattunge*."

Judging by the blatant level of innuendo in Brigit's invitation, I guessed I didn't want to know what "*kattunge*" meant. "I'm good." I batted her hand away from my hair, which she started braiding at random. "My husband doesn't like it when other people touch me." *Back the smack up, girl.*

Brigit cupped my chin, taking in my face before consenting to give me three whole inches of personal space. "Is your husband coming to see us? He puts up a good fight. Strong will." She licked her lips. "Delicious."

"You'll not go near my husband," I warned without wavering. "I'm just here for Jens."

The women atop my boyfriend looked up at me with pleasantly delirious expressions. "Oh, but we've been having such fun with him. Can't he stay?"

"I'm afraid the fun's over, ladies," Jamie said, face red at their nudity and the warm atmosphere that was stiflingly thick with sweat and ickiness. He moved over to Jens, waiting for them to dismount his oiled body. He yanked up his muscular friend, waving me forward to be a crutch for his other slippery side.

I had never seen Jens naked before. My experience with nude men didn't go past the couple of times I'd walked in on Foss getting dressed. My imagination really didn't go past kissing yet, since that was such a new phenomenon for me. To see my boyfriend naked for the first time in a whorehouse was a new low, of which I was already maxed to capacity on. I pulled off the new pouch of lavender powder from around Jens's neck and tossed it on the floor.

"Jens is going to be mad," Jamie warned.

"Oh, his anger's going to be comical compared to mine. Trust me." I snatched his clothing off the floor and helped Jamie drag his heavy body out of The Den of iniquity, ignoring Brigit's invitation for me to stay as long as I wished.

As soon as we hit fresh air, we laid Jens down on the tall grass. I felt painted white inside and hollow to the bone. I didn't realize I was shaking until Jamie's arms went around me after he'd dressed my boyfriend. Jamie pulled me to his chest, squeezing out of me the tears of betrayal that burned as they slithered down my cheeks.

I pulled away and knelt next to Jens, kissing my palm and pressing it to his chest. It was the goodbye kiss I'd never wanted to give him, but he'd earned it fair and square.

Jens wasn't Superman. In the end, Jens was just a man.

5

JENS'S LIES

Somehow we got Jens back to the ship in record time, giving me the distinct impression that Jamie had indeed led us in circles to avoid taking me to The Den.

The plan was to wait until nightfall to start up our journey to Elvage. Bags were packed with the fruits Jamie and I managed to collect on the way back, and anything else we might ever need was secured in Jens's magical red bag.

Jens came to after Mace dropped a bucket of cold water on him and whistled him to semi-wakefulness. His high began to wear off, giving way to a moderate level of lucidity. I stayed out of sight, not wanting to deal with Foss's triumphant jabs at how stupid my relationship with Jens had been, and how naïve I was to expect monogamy from a guy like him who had better things to do than, well, me.

Jens washed off and dressed like a deer in headlights, eyes darting around the ship for signs that I'd seen him like that. He found me half an hour later on the quiet ship, bloodshot eyes and bags under his sweeping lashes that only held deception for me, instead of their usual lure.

Everyone was quietly waiting for my explosion. I would not give it to them.

"Hey, baby," Jens greeted me warily.

"Hey," I answered with forced cheeriness from my spot on the upper deck overlooking the ocean. I glanced at him over my shoulder and shot him a welcoming smile. "You're back. What took you so long?"

Jens's shoulders released a good bit of anxiety at my seeming unawareness of his whereabouts. He moved behind me and placed a kiss on my shoulder as I stood, still facing the ocean. "Nothing important. A few traders weren't up for helping us restock. Took longer than expected. I'm back now, though."

"You feeling okay?"

I could see Jens lightening, thinking he'd not been caught. The whole façade made me sick. The truths he'd told me throughout our entire relationship began to crumble like crusty sand, my castle of truth utterly ruined. "I'm great. A little tired. Ready to get out of here. Did you miss me?" His hand snaked around my stomach. He breathed in the scent of my hair, and sighed contentedly.

I did not cry. I was too devastated feeling his body against mine to register any emotion except crushed. "I missed you. It must've been rough being all alone like that. Jamie told me how he found you. All by yourself, lost in the woods. Scary."

More relief was palpable. "I just spent the whole time thinking about you," he lied.

I forced a light laugh. "That's so funny. Brigit had never even heard of me." He froze against me and stopped breathing. "I had to tell her I was Foss's wife to get you out of The Den." I turned around to face him, stood on my toes and pressed one last kiss to his unmoving lips. "You might want to wash off again. You stink of writhing whore."

With that, I walked away, proud of the way I conducted myself. There was no yelling, not even a fight. Just a clean break that destroyed me where I stood as I put the last few items into my bag.

Jens found me a few minutes later, his gaunt face white with fear. "I'm so sorry. I didn't... it was... Oh, man. I think I'm gonna be sick."

I wanted to punch him in the throat to stop the asinine words. I took a steadying breath, determined to end my first relationship with my first kiss as an adult, not the raving lunatic I wanted to be in that moment. I doubted Martin Luther King was ever in this situation, but if he was, he would have been calm and probably would not have choked the life from the liar.

I pressed a smile to my face I did not feel. "No need for

that. It's my fault. I mean, I wasn't putting out. I understand. You needed things I wasn't ready to give you. Totally acceptable."

"I've never pressured you for anything!" he countered, getting oddly defensive.

I cocked my head to the side and sized him up. "Are you yelling at me?" I asked in a tone that was deadly and quiet. "I don't think you want to do that right now. You're getting off pretty easy here. You've been getting off for over a week now, so you have no reason to yell at me."

Jens placed his hands over his heart, steadying his outburst. "I'm sorry. It wasn't like that. It's not about the girls. I was running low on powder. That's the place to get it around here. I thought I could quit, but..." Panicky tears pricked his eyes before he could suck them back, but they did not fall. "I killed our dog! You're married to Foss! You've got his mark branded on you! I saw something in your kiss, too. Deny it all you want, but it's there! It's a lot to take. I needed something to take the edge off."

My tone was still cool as a cucumber who'd been cheated on by the rotten tomato. "Why are you defending yourself? I'm not mad. I'm not yelling. You can snort whatever you want. You can sleep with whoever you want. You're totally free to be the adult you've always dreamed of. I won't hold you back anymore. It's obvious I was keeping you from doing what you wanted, which is why you lied to me about it. It's fine. It's all fine." I shifted the pack on my back. "Maybe less lying to me, though? It doesn't sit well. I feel like I've earned at least that from you. I kissed Foss while I was accidentally drunk and he was out of his mind, and I told you first thing." I waved my hand around to clarify. "It doesn't matter. You're staying here. I'm traveling with a crapload of people. I don't need you anymore. I can't trust you, so you're free to go back to The Den. I just needed my stuff back, and now I have it."

"That's not how it works, baby," Jens began, stroking the gold tattoo on his cheek.

"My name is Lucy," I snapped, drawing a clear line.

Jens's chest moved unsteadily. "Lucy. That's not how it works. My tattoo is part of your mother's family crest. There's magic in the ink. I'm sworn to your family as long as you're alive, or until I retire. I made that choice years ago to get me away from Bedra. I wasn't expecting to follow you here."

"Oh." *Crap.* "Then I'm sorry I made you get high and go to that orgy. That's on me."

"You know it's not."

I forced a fake smile to try and make light of the crushing situation. "It's not exactly how I imagined seeing you naked for the first time, you know? I always pictured it without other women on top of you and me without my guts ripped out all over the floor for your adoring fans to trip over. Not as fun your way. For me, anyway."

He touched his stomach. "I'm going to be sick."

"I turned my first boyfriend to magical heroine," I said in monotone, jerking both thumbs to my chest. "I rock."

"You didn't do this!"

"Well, someone has to take responsibility, and you don't seem up for it." I shook my head. "Whatever. Stay here or don't." I gave him a brave smile, but refused to look him in the eye. I knew if I did, I'd be lost. I'd either break down and cry in front of him or I'd want him back. Neither of those were options. "Excuse me." Without another word, I moved to the stairwell where everyone else was discreetly hiding from the explosion that had yet to happen.

"Come on, Loos! Get mad at me! Throw a fit! Hit me! Something!" he begged. "Don't leave it like this. Don't leave!"

I turned, determined not to get emotional. "Why should I be mad? You explained it all pretty well once you stopped lying like a fool. You're addicted to drugs, and the only way to get the good kind is from the whorehouse. Why would I be mad about that? Seems logical."

He pulled at his hair, his nose red from emotion. "I'm so sorry! You have to know how much I hate the way I am! I wish I could take it back, Loos! You have no idea!"

I kept the agony off my face. No matter what, I would end my first adult relationship as an adult. He would be the screaming child who followed his vices to his undoing. I would be calm and get on with my life. I kept my shoulders level and my voice pleasantly calm. "Oh, Jens. You're fine. Enjoy your life and your choices. But leave me to get on with mine. Not to sound snobby, but I think I'm worth a guy I don't have to push naked women off of. Maybe I'm old-fashioned, but I think I'll hold out for someone who doesn't lie to me or have to get high to deal with his life if I'm in it." I pursed my lips together. "Don't you think I deserve that?"

"Of course you do, babe."

"Lucy," I corrected him, my tone mutating to steel in an instant.

He nodded, wringing his hands and wiping the sweat from his palms onto his jeans. "Lucy. You deserve more than me, but I need you. I waited so long for you. I slipped up once! Once! I've cut back so much since we got together!"

I addressed his chest, unwilling to look into his emerald eyes that were begging me to stay. I looked down at myself, marveling at how different I felt than when I started off in Undra with him as my guide. "I'm all grown up now, thanks to you. First kiss. First relationship. First breakup. First whorehouse. I think this is where I ripcord off the train." I turned from him to leave, but Jens had other plans.

In no less than two seconds, he cleared the distance between us, spun me around and cupped my face in the hands I used to find comfort in. He kissed me. Over and over, he tried to draw me out and force me to feel how good we had been together. It was passionate and full of all the things I loved about him, laced with a note of begging.

It was cruel.

"Stop!" I cried, finally letting my volume climb to a pathetic bleat of agony. "You made your choice!" I took a deep breath to steady my trembling hands and lowered my volume to a whisper before continuing. "Goodbye, Jens."

6

HORRIBLE AS I WAS

There was a darkness around me, and not just because we traveled only at night. I could feel it as we walked on the outskirts of Bedra. Foss was too well-known, so Jens kept his hand on his shoulder, vanishing them both. It was just as well. Jens didn't want to be seen, and I needed a break from seeing him. Most relationships were granted the mercy of distance once ended. Like everything else I needed in life, mercy just wasn't around for me.

I walked beside my uncle in silence. Everyone respected the mood and kept mostly to themselves. It made for a tense journey, but a quiet one, so it wasn't too bad.

By the time the sun began to rise, we were all exhausted. We were still a few days away from Elvage, and since Jens had not secured supplies on his trip to single-hood, food was getting scarce.

Foss spoke from behind me. "We need food and a few things from the market. I can't go, obviously, but Lucy, you've got control of my estate. You can buy what we need."

I nodded, putting the pack I'd just taken off back on. My spine groaned. "Fine. Where is it?"

"I'll take you," Jens volunteered.

"No, thanks. What does everyone need?" I took orders like a waitress, noticing Jens asked for nothing. "Come on, Jamie." I waved my laplanded buddy forward, taking a step in what I hoped was the right direction. I did not look back to confirm he followed, only trusted he would catch up if he didn't want a headache.

"Wait up, Lucy," Jamie called, trotting closer. "I'm so tired. I know you are too."

"Let's make it quick, then. Do you know where we're going?" The oversized tropical plants were hard to navigate through, being as short as I was. Walking on the sandy beaches all through the night had been hard, but this was even more challenging. The grass was up to my chest, and in some spots climbed even higher.

"The nearest market isn't too far. Ten-minute walk north. Five if you hop on my back," he hinted.

"I'm fine. I can do it." I knew I was being stubborn, but Jamie was too polite to call me on it. I felt him tap on the wall of my brain, a little passageway that linked me to him.

I locked the door to keep him out. He didn't need a glimpse at the wreckage. "Stop for a second." I batted away the grass so I could look up at him properly. "Look, what you did by covering for Jens isn't cool. I get that he's your bro, but I deserve to know what's going on in my own relationship. I think I've earned the right to a little honesty from you. Don't make me go poking around in your head to see if you're constantly lying to me."

Jamie lowered his head. "I'm sorry. You're right. Britta wanted to tell you, but I knew you would break up with him. You're good for him, Lucy. Jens needs someone like you. You speak the same language. Even though he grew up in Tonttu, he's never found his place with our people."

"Then when we get over to my side, you can find him a nice prostitute drug dealer to sleep with all the livelong day. I'm a queen here, but I'm a dime a dozen on the Other Side. You'll see. He'll find someone else. Point is, don't lie to me. Foss is a hormonal jerk, I'm still getting used to Mace, and Uncle Rick is always a flight risk. Britt's great, but I don't expect her to fink on her brother. You and I are stuck together for the long haul. Don't make life suck even more for me. Don't screw me over like that again."

Jamie nodded, contrite. "Yes, ma'am."

I tromped forward, exhausted both physically and emotionally. Beneath the scarring, I felt a small glimmer of pride in myself. I really had grown.

Jamie led the way to the market, which was smaller than the one in Fossegrim, but had everything we needed.

I flashed my ring to the female-driven commerce, catching both looks of admiration and ones of jealousy that I'd bagged the almighty Foss. Whatever. They could have him and Jens.

I bought Jamie a pack and stuffed it full of food that was not biscuits. My pack was filled with everything else. I eyed a vendor that sold lavender powder products. She had drug-infused body oils, bread baked with the stuff, and various other items that caught my eye. I left Jamie's side and made a beeline for the booth, fingering a small vial of the vice that had ruined my relationship. It was a glass tube with a blue swirl winding around it like a pretty little serpent.

"How much?" I asked the woman with so much black smudge around her eyes, she looked like a raccoon with boobs.

"Thirty." She addressed my necklace with wonder. "You're Foss's wife?"

"Yup."

"Take it. And please send my regards. I'm Dagmar." She lowered her voice. "He bought my sister years ago. I never charge him for anything. I'm indebted to him for taking care of her." She leaned over the table and grabbed my arm. "Erika. Is she well?"

My heart lurched at mention of the friend I'd left behind. Tonya Part Two, the Amish Edition. "She is. She's happy there. Laughs a lot and is super cool. She's been a good friend to me."

"Send her my love. If Master Foss needs any more slaves, he can have me. I'm not Mare, and neither is she. We just live amongst them. Please mention me to your husband. Please." She clung to me, her darkened eyes begging me for a way out.

I nodded. "I'll tell her you miss her, and that you've got a great shop here. And really, Foss can pay you for this." I placed the vial in my pocket. "Take the full price off his account. I insist."

"No, no. Thank you. Just knowing Erika is alive and well is enough for me."

I detached myself from Dagmar and turned to find Jamie standing behind me with a dour expression I tried to ignore. "What are you doing?" he demanded.

"Shopping like the ditz I am. That's everything, right?"

"Put that back."

I pushed past him, heading back the way we came. Jamie followed after me, and I could feel frustration radiating off him. He banged on the door to our shared brainwaves, but I kept it shut tight, ignoring his impatient calls for me to let him in. Once we reached the ridiculously tall grass that offered us some separation from the commerce, he grabbed my shoulder.

I shook him off. "Get away from me," I growled, not wishing to have a big discussion with him.

"Stop! You can't take that, Lucy."

"Actually, I can. My darling husband paid for it, or I tried to pay for it, anyway. I don't actually need your permission to buy street legal drugs. You're not my dad. You're not my fake husband. You're not my boyfriend. You're not my brother. We're barely friends from the way you covered for your boy and screwed me over like you did. Don't act all concerned now. I won't try any while we're still on the job. I can control myself. I'll wait till it's all over to bliss out." I touched the tiny container in my pocket. "It'll affect you zero."

His hands cast out in exasperation. "It'll get me high, too! Everything you do affects me."

Crap. "Well, I'll do it while you're sleeping, then. You won't feel a thing."

"Why? You saw what it's done to Jens. It's ruined his life!"

"Why?" I echoed in utter flabbergast. "Huh, I wasn't expecting to have to pick just one reason. Let me think which is the best one. And I won't even use the whole 'my family's dead' card." My arms banded around my stomach to hold my guts inside. "I have to know there's a promise it'll all stop someday. I need that, Jamie. Just having this in my pocket, I already feel better." I stroked my pocket over the vial. "It's my ripcord. Without this, it's only more pain. More of everyone dying. More fighting. More never being alone, thanks to you and my adulterous shadow, and still always being alone *because* of you and my adulterous shadow." I shrugged and gave a glib laugh. "Who's going to want to be with me when I come with you two?"

Jamie looked like I had slapped him, and I instantly felt

bad. "I'm not trying to be in your way, Lucy. I didn't plan to get laplanded with my best friend's girlfriend."

I held up my hands in surrender. "I know. I'm sorry. That was below the belt. I didn't mean it. Well, I did, but it was cruel to say. Let's just truce it out and get through this. I won't touch the powder until after the last portal falls and we're settled somewhere. Promise." I drew an X over my heart to prove my sincerity. "I need something I can count on to take the pain away. I can't explain it better than that. I just need it. I've got nothing left, Jamie."

Horrible as I was, Jamie wrapped his arms around me. The tall grass shrouded our embrace, giving me the smallest breath of respite against his always steady heart. "Okay, sweetheart. Okay. Just don't touch it until it's all over. Then can we talk about it again before you try it? Who knows? You might not need it by then."

We walked back to the others, and I was glad I missed the whole setting up camp ordeal. I'd bought six tents back in Fossegrim, but only three survived the bout with the farlig fisk. They were two-man tents, and when divvying up sleeping arrangements, I was the odd man out.

"Come on." Jens beckoned me to the tent he was sharing with Foss. "We don't have to talk if you don't want. Just come sleep here."

I shook my head. "I'm keeping watch. I'm not tired."

"There's nothing to watch for. There aren't any real threats in Bedra this far out from civilization."

"I'm fine here." I sat against a thick palm tree that bore

pink mangoes, staking out my territory. It wouldn't be easy to sleep outside in the daylight, but I couldn't imagine a situation in which I'd rest peacefully anytime soon.

Jens was in pain watching me from afar, as he'd done for years before I'd been introduced to him. He looked like someone who'd just gone on a bender. "You don't want to be around me. I get it. Then take my spot. I'll sleep out there."

"Please," I said, rubbing my eyes. "You look like you've been hit with a truck. Get some rest."

"Lucy," he pled.

"No, Jens. Just go to bed. I don't have it in me to deal with you right now. It's been a day."

I turned my head from his long stare until he finally retreated to the tent he shared with Foss. I tried to make myself comfortable against the tree, but let's face it, it's a tree. A few minutes later, the tent Mace shared with Uncle Rick opened. My brother poked his head out and beckoned me forward. "In you get," he said, leading me to lay down in between them. Uncle Rick shifted over to make room, but there really wasn't any. Mace laid down and hugged me. As soon as his arms secured themselves around me, he rolled onto his back, tucking me into his wiry nook. "There. Go to sleep, *kära*."

I blinked back the tears I wanted to cry all over his black shirt and sucked in my heartbreak as best I could. Uncle Rick patted my head with a weighted hand before drifting off to almost-sleep.

"Do you want me to make you sleep with a whistle? That's an easy one." Mace whispered, rubbing my back in a way I could not help but feel relaxed by.

"No. I'm too susceptible to you. I might never wake up if you do that."

"Lucy," Uncle Rick mumbled, "tell your brother I'll turn him into a toad if you two don't go to sleep. I'm an old man. I need my rest."

Despite myself, I giggled. He'd said the exact same thing to Linus and me many times when we were keeping him up after he put us to bed during his monthly babysitting visits.

The thought of Linus did not comfort me as I hoped it would. Neither did Mace's tenderness or the sound of nature doing its thing outside the tent. My life with my family felt eons away now. I'd changed so much since then. I wondered if Linus would even recognize me anymore, short hair aside.

I fell asleep to the sound of Uncle Rick's soft snores and the gentle thrumming of Mace's heartbeat.

7

CONFUSION AND COMFORT

The sound of rustling woke me only seconds before something heavy as an ox rolled on my arm that had fallen lax off Mace's stomach. "Ah! What the crap?" I pushed the wrestling oxen off me and stumbled out of the tent. The thing that had landed on me was the third tent, occupied by Foss and Jens, who were apparently dueling inside the tiny space. "Knock it off, you two!" I yelled, rubbing my sore arm. Mace, Alrik, Britta and Jamie scrambled out of their tents with wild blinking eyes.

Foss's response was forced through his effort to best Jens. "He's detoxing! Mace! Help me out with your whistle!"

Mace threw his head back, dismayed at the scene as the two bears tumbled around the campsite. Jens was sweaty from head to toe and positively ashen with fear on his face.

"Get off him, Foss!" I shouted, backing up as the two fought for dominance. They were fairly evenly matched. Foss was bigger, but Jens was a seasoned fighter.

"Cover your ears!" Charles commanded everyone. He waited for me to comply before letting out a low solitary note that sucked the fight out of Jens. He collapsed lifelessly to the ground, as if a hypnotist had counted down from three.

I was paralyzed as Alrik checked Jens's pupils and tested his forehead to feel his burning temperature. He shook his head, silently scolding the sleeping man.

Foss stood from the white sand, stretching his back and cracking his neck. "He's sleeping out here tonight. I'm not sharing a tent with him while he's sweating out the poison."

Jamie and Britta looked down at Jens in pity before returning to their tent as if nothing crazy had just occurred.

"Hello! What was that? What just happened?" I demanded, staring down at the snoring Jens at my feet.

Mace rubbed the sleep from his eyes and stretched. "Jens just spent a week with the Mare. They sit on your chest and take your will, replacing it with demons that chase you in your sleep until all the powder's out of your system. Jens hasn't been totally clean in a long time. He's always snorting something to get by. He'll have a couple rough nights, and then he'll be back to normal." Mace bent over and touched his toes. "Well, whatever his normal will be without the powder as a crutch." He yawned after Uncle Rick went back into his tent and laid down. "Come on, baby."

I froze, staring at him like a deer in headlights. "What?"

Charles caught his mistake too late, his shoulders going rigid. "I'm tired. I didn't mean to call you that."

Foss watched the exchange as he nursed a wound on his bicep.

"It's fine," I said, waving off the horrifying faux pas as if it meant nothing. "Go on ahead. I'll stay out here and keep an eye on Jens. I'm not tired."

Mace noticed my shift away from him, and his mood deflated. "It was an accident, Lucy. A little slip. That's all. I know you're my sister."

"Oh, I know. No big deal. I was just a little cramped in there. That's all. Go on to sleep, baby," I teased him, trying to make things less awkward.

Mace's tail drooped. He cast me a melancholy smile and disappeared inside his tent next to Alrik.

Foss stared me down until I met his gaze. He nodded twice and jerked his head toward his tent, motioning for me to come inside.

I stepped over Jens, who was laying with his mouth open on his back across the white sand, and tried not to feel sorry for him. Foss pushed me inside. I hugged the canvas wall and sat with my knees to my chest to give him plenty of room. Silently, he laid on his side facing me, and then dragged me down by my kneecap to lay next to him.

In a gesture of unexpected kindness, Foss cradled me in his arms. "Go ahead. Let it out."

The dam I had constructed the moment I saw the naked women straddling my boyfriend broke all over Foss. My tears streamed down my nose and cheeks, wetting his bare chest. "I want to go home," I whimpered. "I just want to go home."

"I know. Me, too."

Foss was always warm and cold at the same time. If his skin felt warm, he acted cold. Tonight, he was chilly, but his temperament was warm. Well, his version of warm, anyway. I wrapped my free arm around his ribs and rubbed his back, forcing friction where he needed it on his spine. He relaxed, closing his eyes and leaning his forehead to mine. "Get some sleep, baby," he joked.

"Shut up, darling husband." I smiled through my tears, and Foss wiped a few away.

I fell asleep in my enemy's arms, loathing my life, but clinging to the moments of rest he provided.

8

PILLOW TALK

The next few days were much the same. We traveled by night and slept during the day. I kept quiet, sticking to the "speak when spoken to" rule that never failed me. I took extra care to keep the psychic wall up between Jamie and me, speaking to him only in sleep when he needed to escape into my brain from his horrifying nightmares.

The guys planned Alrik's approach to the portal that would surely be guarded, and Britta and Jamie were paired off in their sweet little love bubble. I was happy for them, but my misery over my own failed attempt at a love life was palpable. I tried not to pine. I kept myself tucked tight inside Foss's tent and did not go to Jens when his night terrors from the Mares plagued him.

Foss and I reached an understanding. He stopped being so mean to me, and I slept next to him. I learned a lot about him during our dismal slumber parties. I learned that he was a jerk who liked to insult his bedmate right before falling asleep. One morning I fell asleep to his jeer of "Don't expect me to hold you tonight. I've had enough of you today." I awoke to find his arm around me, and my body scooped to his chest.

The next morning was something like, "If you open your mouth even once, you'll regret it. I don't want to hear what you think of Alrik's stupid plan. I know it's a bad idea. I've already said as much. They're going through with it anyway. Deal with it."

"I didn't say a thing about the plan! You have no idea what I think. Leave me alone." I rolled on my side away from him, curled up in my usual fetal position and tried to force sleep upon me in the daylight. What I wouldn't give for a sleep mask. And earplugs. Heck, if I'm asking for things, I'd like a bed, too.

Foss snapped back, "You've been doing that quiet thing all day. I know when you want to say something, but you do that annoying polite thing. I know you think we're walking into a deathtrap."

My arms flew out as I spoke with probably too much vehemence. Foss always managed to make me irritable. "First I'm not allowed to talk. Then I'm annoying because I didn't argue with anyone today and kept my mouth shut? Make up your mind, psycho! Pick a fight with someone else. I'm exhausted."

"You're exhausted? I'm the one who killed and cooked those kanins."

My purple tank top clung to me in uncomfortable places. It was so hot and humid out, and I only had jeans and long dresses to choose from. I'd bathed in the ocean, but the humidity kept us all sweaty.

I rolled my eyes at Foss as I tugged at a damp spot on my back. "Yes. You own the rights to all sleepiness. If you're tired, no one else is allowed to be. You are the king of all things that suck the life out of people." I brushed the hair from my face and started talking with my hands even more. "Forget that it takes two or three of my steps to equal just one of yours. Forget that I'm the one who climbed four trees today so we could have those pink mangoes."

"For the last time, they're called *persikas*!"

I let out a noise of frustration. "You're so infuriating! Next time I'm acting as Queen Lucy of the Other Side, I'm having you guillotined first thing just so I can get some peace and quiet! And you mumbling about the clouds all evening? What are we supposed to do about clouds? What would you like me to do about the clouds? I mean, on a personal and metaphysical level, what powers do you think I have?"

"If you had the power to shut up, I'd be happy."

Alrik called from his tent. "Goodnight, children."

I closed my mouth, angry that Foss riled me up just before the promise of rest. I held my stomach and squeezed my eyes shut, praying for a well-aimed lightning bolt to hit right next to me.

"I can feel you seething," Foss griped.

"Can you feel me kicking your hairy butt? Because it's coming. Shut up and go to sleep."

After a few more choice words from both of us, Jamie reminded me through our bond that Foss had just lost everything, and he was surly on his best day. I pushed Jamie out of my brain. I closed my eyes and ignored Foss as he tried to verbally jab me a few more times just to have someone to fight with and blame for the loss of his grand life.

Finally I turned to face him, my eyes tired and my will to fight dwindling. Without speaking, I kissed my finger and pressed it to his scowl. "Shh."

He clutched my wrist tight in his fist, his anger always frightening. He stared me down for several seconds, deciding between bear and puppy dog.

I scooted closer, begging him with my eyes not to strike. I wound my free arm under his head, bringing him to my chest in a hug he would never admit to needing.

He softened against his will and melted into my embrace, thank goodness. His finger poked through the ring at my sternum. He examined the gem he'd worn his entire adult life, and all the promise it held that was now lost.

Wordlessly he pulled back and touched the scar of his mark on my breastbone, then looked at me with apologetic eyes that held none of the malice he addressed me with earlier. My fingernails scraped along his scalp, making him sigh contentedly above me. He moved his hands underneath my ribs and lifted a couple inches so my chest was elevated. I was too baffled to react as he lowered his face to just above my cleavage and kissed the scar with more gentleness than I guessed he was capable of.

The intimacy between us was so confusing; I wasn't sure how to react. I had goose bumps all over, and could hear my heartbeat pounding in my ears in time with the ocean lapping a few meters away from our camp on the beach.

Foss chuckled quietly at my wide eyes. "Don't worry. I still hate you."

"Whew!" I whispered. "I thought you up and lost your mind for a second there."

"No. Not yet, anyways. Jens can have you the second you stop pretending you'll never forgive him." He rolled me on my side facing away from him and pulled me to his front, spooning me before I could punch him. Or thank him. I really wasn't sure what just happened. "Goodnight, lovely wife." He reached for his sheathed knife and hugged me with it, pressing the cool leather to my chest. The closeness of the blade terrified me, but it also made me feel somehow safer. That's the thing about Foss.

My voice was small as I reached over my head to pat his cheek. "Goodnight, darling husband. Maybe ease up on the crazy pills tomorrow."

Foss laughed softly as he kissed my wrist, and I could feel him relax against my back. However it happened, we were becoming friends. There had to be worse things than that. I couldn't name any, but I'm sure there were plenty. I closed my eyes against the shiver I felt when Foss pressed his lips to the sensitive spot behind my ear.

9

LET IT RAIN

I awoke to Foss rolling around in his sleep. His arm was still under me, but the rest of his body was shifting around, trying to find comfort on the uneven ground. The sheathed knife had fallen to the ground as he tossed.

I turned over and touched his chest, hoping to bring some peace to his sleep. His other arm was flung over his forehead, but at my touch, it swung out and knocked me in the jaw. "Ow!" I complained. I heard Jamie's tent rustling, and knew he'd been roused, too.

Foss came to, groggy, but able to piece together what he'd done easily enough as he picked up his sheathed dagger again. "Oh! Sorry. I didn't mean to hit you that time."

"That time," I scoffed, rubbing the sore spot with a

frown. "Maybe you should try not hitting people on purpose or on accident. Novel concept, I know."

"I said I was sorry. Come here. Let me look at it." He squinted in the dim light at my face, scoffing at the nothing that greeted him. "You're such a baby."

"I didn't say you wounded me for life. You just banged me, is all. I'm allowed to say ouch."

"Go back to sleep. I promise to wait till you're awake to hit you again."

"Ha. Ha. You're hilarious." I settled into his nook, which was surprisingly comfortable, despite his bulk. I missed Jens, and welcomed the man Band-Aid Foss provided. "It's getting dark," I commented, allowing him to lift my leg to wrap around his as he shifted on his back. "I miss sleeping in the dark."

"Yeah? I miss it when you used to be quiet. Let's go back to that." He kissed my lips once, and my heart jumped at the contact. His eyes were closed already, and his breathing leveled off in a matter of minutes. I reasoned that he probably hadn't meant to kiss me, and decided not to examine the oddity. His restfulness lulled me, and I drifted off to sleep in his arms, my hand finding respite on his navel.

I dreamt of Jens. That was no surprise. My waking and sleeping brainwaves were often plagued with equal thoughts of missing him and being angry at him.

The two planes of consciousness converged when Jens ripped open the tent flap and gasped at Foss and I wrapped around each other. I sat up, remembering I had nothing to be ashamed of.

His expression was hard as he looked into my eyes, hurt slashed across his face. "A storm's rolling in. I can go in one of the other tents, if you want."

I shook my head. "Come on in. You're fine." I tried to wake up more fully, pulling my knees to my chest so Jens could sit next to me. It was awkward being near him, and darn near impossible to relax with two huge men in the cramped tent.

No sooner had Jens fastened the ties on the tent flap did the rain begin to fall. There was about ten seconds of pitter patter before the heavens opened and dumped buckets of water down on us. "Um, is this normal?" I asked, gathering my backpack to me just in case we needed to bolt.

Jens looked at the roof warily. "For this region? It's not unheard of for it to pour like this for days. Bedra has rain like your world doesn't see all that often. We'll see how this tent holds up. Don't touch the sides if you can help it."

"Yup." There was a stint one summer that we traveled like nomads to different state parks. I could tear down a two-man tent with one hand tied behind my back after that.

"Go back to sleep," Jens suggested. "I didn't mean to interrupt your... whatever that was."

Foss spoke without opening his eyes. He was not ready to give up his claim on half the space in the overcrowded area. "Come on, lovely wife. You heard him. Lay back down next to your big, strong, half-naked husband." He chuckled at his ability to stir the pot without even having to be fully awake.

Jens punched Foss hard in the thigh. "Knock it off! I'm miserable enough as it is."

Foss grabbed his leg. "Ah! I was kidding!"

"Me, too. I punched your leg as a joke. Get it? Every time you ask to be hit, I slug you. Fun game. I think I'm winning."

Foss sat up and rubbed out the sting. "You're not used to living with the aches and pains of your job. Bound to make you a little irritable at first. Stay clean, though. The worst has already passed."

Jens ignored Foss completely. "Do you think we should stay here?"

"For now. At least as long as the tents hold up."

As if on cue, Jamie and Britta announced frantically that water was seeping in and pooling in their tent. *Tell Jens we're packing up. Time to move.*

"Jamie's breaking down his tent. What happens next?" I asked, zipping my backpack shut.

"Here. I'll take your bag. Your stuff won't get wet if it's inside my pack." Jens kept his eyes from mine as he shoved my stuff inside his red bag, then did the same with Foss's and cinched it shut. "We tear our tent down and see how far we can get on foot."

Thunder crashed so loud, I let out a noise of alarm. It

sounded like we were inside a bowling alley, only amplified to the point of an uncomfortable decibel level. I clapped my hands over my ears after I scrambled out of the tent after Jens.

The ocean was in uproar. Waves that seemed so far away when we were inside the tent were near and huge. The shore was being eaten away by the zealous ocean, inching closer to our camp with every crash.

Foss broke down the tent in record time, rolling it up and hoisting it up by the shoulder strap that made it easy to carry and a good buy when I was tent shopping for the group. Jens had Alrik's tent over his shoulder, and Jamie had his. We were set to run, but had nowhere to go. We were running out of shore to travel along, as most of it was being confiscated by the ten-foot tall waves that made a scream catch in my throat. I'd been surfing a few times before when we lived in California. These waves were nothing like those. Angry, enormous and fast, I could not imagine fielding my way through those on a simple board.

"Inland!" Jens shouted over another crash of thunder I could feel in my teeth. He grabbed onto my hand and ran with me toward the too-tall grass that showed no signs of bowing to the weather.

The ocean was set on a slight incline from the mainland. As we stomped through the thick foliage that climbed to my neck in some parts, the water began to pool around our ankles.

And then our knees.

The rural part of Bedra we were in was flooding, and I was wading through water up to my chest before I knew it. The guys had their packs over their heads as we trudged toward what we hoped was safety, and then everyone shoved their packs inside Jens's for safe keeping. Talk about a flash flood. We seemed to be in some sort of basin that was a magnet for torrential rain. I gave up on walking and started swimming.

My foot caught on a branch or a vine or a root or something, and suddenly I was submerged. I tugged and tugged against the loop that snagged me, but it would not let me go. Panic set in for a few seconds until it dawned on me that if I died this way, it would be okay with me. There were worse ways to go, and I had precious little to fight the root for. It probably had more to live for than I did. I gave the loop another obligatory jiggle, and then let the water take me. Aside from the burning in my lungs, it was actually pretty peaceful in the suffocating quiet. Flashbacks of the Nøkkendalig made my body feel like it was on fire, but I tried to forget about that so my last moments wouldn't be such a horror.

Jamie was screaming in my head, but I mentally shrugged. I tried to free myself, but I couldn't. *Oh, well.* Twenty years was a decent amount of time to live. What was I really going to do with a few more years?

Hands yanked at me, twisting my ankle painfully. I slapped at the grip that felt rough, like Foss's. Water began to enter my lungs, and I thought I might burst from the agonizing burn.

Fingers I would know anywhere unwrapped my ankle from the vine and brought me to the surface. I'd spent a long time studying Jens's hands.

Uncle Rick covered my mouth and sucked out the water, while Mace did the same for Jamie. Charles acted as Jamie's crutch to move him forward.

Jens wrapped my arms around his neck and stuck me to his front. "Hold on tight! There's elevation just up ahead." He pointed, but I could barely see more than two feet in front of me. The rain was terribly thick, and the sun had gotten sick of the weather and deserted us completely. The moon was also wussing out, providing the bare minimum of light through the forest of storm clouds.

I clung to Jens, wrapping my functioning leg around his waist. He was strong, and despite myself, I allowed the comfort I missed to seep through my soaked clothes and into my hollow chest. His presence ripped at my torn heart while simultaneously filling in the shredded bits. It was all very befuddling, and my ankle hurt like a beast.

We hit a deep pocket, and everyone except for Foss was forced to swim. With great reluctance, Jens hoisted me up and placed me on Foss's shoulders. He stayed next to us the entire way, treading water as Foss stalked onward, gripping my shins so I did not wash away in the current that was starting to form.

Britta was screaming as she swam, echoes of the

Nøkkendalig too much to fend off, even with the distraction of torrential rain. The mournful cry clawed at my sanity, forcing a whimper from me as we moved through the water. Foss stroked my knee to calm me, which ironically, only made me weep harder. I couldn't handle any acknowledgment of my pain or fear; it only made the hands feel more permanent on my body.

My ankle was definitely going to be a handicap. Just touching it against Foss's side was more pain than I could handle gracefully. I bit my lip and whimpered as we trudged toward a point I could not see.

10

MANIAC CANNIBALS

W hen we reached "elevation", which only lowered the water to their chins, they all cast around for higher ground, but no one could see very far.

The rain was fat and oppressive, jabbing at me so hard, I was afraid the drops might actually knock me out at some point. We were far off our course, but that was neither here nor there at this point. Survival was paramount, and the storm was only getting worse.

Since I was the tallest for the moment, I cupped my hands around my eyes and cast around for anything out of the inclement weather.

"That way!" I called. The nearest point of safety was far, but it was all we had to shoot for. "There's a mountain up ahead. It's the only thing not underwater."

We could barely see or hear each other, so I used the

link to tell Jamie we all needed to hold hands and move against the building current forward toward that mountain. Everyone linked up and waded through the storm together. Somehow through everything we'd all been through, we'd learned to work as a team.

The swelling victory was short-lived. Nature decided that rain was not enough punishment. A cold wind gusted through the plains that was so strong, trees were bending. I was mostly out of the water, and I shivered violently at the arctic chill in the tropical land.

One tree decided it had enough. The trunk snapped in two, making an ominous cracking sound that was loud enough to warn us through the chaos. "Duck under it!" I commanded as the tree was shoved with the current right toward us, ready to clothesline everyone in the chest.

This was a good plan until I realized that when Foss ducked instead of lying flat, it put me right in the way of the tree. I screamed as I floated, and just before the trunk was ready to knock me off my perch, Jamie pressed on my chest and dunked me backwards. The tree scraped over my front, ripping and gouging as it passed over my face.

When we all resurfaced, I could feel warm blood running down my cheek. I looked over at Jamie and gasped at the phantom wounds that mirrored my own. Our forehead and left cheek was scraped up enough to be bleeding, and I could feel my torso and hipbone burning.

"We're okay!" Jamie shouted above the din to reassure me.

I nodded and blinked blood and rain out of my eyes. I found our destination and pointed forward. "That way!" Everyone linked hands again, and we fought against the current and debris with valiant effort, with me at the helm. It felt good to be useful, and when we finally reached the mountain after an entire hour of fighting with the weather for each step, I was grateful I had not led everyone on a fool's errand. The mountain was a welcome respite with plenty of footholds to grab onto, and even a convenient little plateau with a cave and an overhang not too far up.

It was hard to climb when everyone and everything was so wet. Our clothes were heavy as bricks, but Britta and Mace managed to make it up the slope without falling. Jens pushed Alrik up and held out his hands underneath him until the older man was out of the water and safely on his way to his surrogate son.

Foss tugged on my leg, the water now only to his knees as he stood atop a rock at the base of the mountain. "Can you climb?"

I nodded, knowing it was a lie. "Yeah. Put me down and go on ahead."

Jamie shook his head. "Our ankle's busted. No way are we scaling a mountain on it. I've been hopping or swimming the whole way."

"The rope from your pack," I suggested. We were so beaten down by the rain, but so close to our goal. I wasn't giving up now just because I couldn't scale a mountain. Details, details.

Jens fished around and yanked out a rope from the ship he'd packed just in case. We shouted the plan up to Alrik, who caught the end on the third try. Jamie wrapped his end around his forearm and climbed as best he could on one foot, using mostly upper body strength to move toward safety. We both cried out when he slipped on the rock, our bad ankle banging pain up our leg. "We're okay, Jamie!" I called to him. "You can do it!" Foss rubbed my calf and kissed the inner part of my kneecap.

Mace, Britta and Alrik tugged Jamie up the last few steps, and I heaved a gust of relief for him.

"I can take her," Jens said, turning to Foss. "No way is she making that climb. Jamie barely survived it."

Foss waved off Jens's offer, taking the handicap as a challenge. "Wait behind us in case she slips off." He lowered me from his shoulders to his back and gripped the rock, testing his balance with me pulling him backward. "Hang on tight," he warned me.

Jens and Foss were natural climbers. They were natural everything, really. But as Foss hoisted us out of the water, every step upward was met with either a grunt or a noise of frustration. I could not imagine how strenuous it must have been for him to climb with all the obstacles, plus me on his back.

When he finally gripped the plateau, Mace and Alrik tugged me upward off of Foss so he could hoist himself over the edge. Jens followed soon after, and when we were all safe, they all made their way into the shallow cavern that provided much-needed shelter from the storm. Everyone panted and collapsed on the floor, adrenaline surging as I tried to join them. Jamie had been dragged to the back of the cave, and I tried to crawl, but my body rebelled, my arms buckling.

Foss pushed himself off the plateau and picked me up like the useless rag doll I was. He carried me into the shelter and away from the rain that pelted us in painful places. "Here. Take this," he murmured to Jens as he handed me down to sit in Jens's lap.

I cried on Jens's bare shoulder. The rain, the Nøkkendalig and my many injuries all stacked atop each other, crushing me where I sat. Jens was breathing heavy, but despite his fatigue, he held me tight, kissing my face every few seconds to make the most of my presence in his embrace.

The relief of having made it through the storm mingled with the rush of being back in Jens's arms. Before I knew it, I was kissing him. He tasted like rain and the most delicious man I'd ever been near. I devoured him, his relief and testosterone swelling at my break on our stalemate. I tugged on his hair and kissed him hard, our lips sucking and teeth nipping as we clung to each other's wet bodies. He ran his hand under the bottom of my tank top and clutched my back. My body was both freezing and on fire, and the only thing I needed was more of whatever addicted me to him so. I ran my hands over his bare chest and clawed at his shoulders, wishing there was a way to be physically closer than skin-to-skin. I could not get close enough, nor could I satiate the desire that burned inside me.

Each kiss only added more accelerant to my furnace, until somehow we were writhing against each other on the floor at the back of the cave. He pinned my arms above my head and kissed a line down my neck, sucking on the skin and biting like an animal as he climbed his way back up to my mouth. We kissed like maniac cannibals trying to tear at each other just to make certain it was real. That we were real. That we would not be swept away by anything other than each other ever again.

The others were too exhausted to pay us much mind as we temporarily made up without the use of words.

11

JENS RUNNING AWAY

The next three days were spent in the cave as it continued to rain. It was close quarters, so we all tried to be extra polite. Foss's version of that was going completely silent, which was a vast improvement on his usual personality.

It was a good thing we had no avenue of escape. Jamie and I needed time to heal. Alrik needed time to work out the bugs in his suicidal plan for the Elvage portal. And Jens and I just needed time.

The cavern was small. Only four meters by four for six large people and one me. Still, there was a small nook in the back corner that curved off in the dark. It was just enough room for Jens to sit down and pull me onto his lap. We whispered in our tapered off area and made out like teenagers for hours. We slept curled around each other, stuffed in the back, away from view of the others. Though I could tell

Mace was annoyed that I'd apparently forgiven Jens so soon, everyone else enjoyed the extra space we left them by being on top of each other all the time out of sight. I threw up a solid wall in my mind to keep Jamie out, but every now and then when I was swept up in Jens, Jamie politely reminded me to put it back up so he didn't have to see our reunion.

We did not talk about The Den. Jens tried to bring it up a few more times, but I shushed him. "I'm not ready to deal with that right now. Let's just get through this. End the portals and go home. We can set up a normal life and go to couple's counseling after that. I'll be really mad then. Promise."

"You can really do that?"

"Compartmentalization is my super power. You've got invisibility, and I can deal with intense emotional trauma. No trading."

"Loos, I'm so sorry. I'll never touch the stuff again. I haven't used since you and Jamie brought me back. Longest I've been clean in a long time."

"Good for you." I wanted to feel super proud of him, and part of me probably was, but I kept picturing the naked women sucking the fight out of him. "I still don't trust you."

He nodded solemnly, donning his gulping-a-spoonful-of-medicine face. "That's fair. Anything I can do?"

I traced a line down his bare chest. "Keep your shirt off to distract me from plotting your inevitable demise."

He chuckled, flexing his bicep for my benefit. "Done. Though the other guys gave up on shirts a while ago, too. Not sure that gives me the edge I need." He kissed me, not able to make it more than a few sentences before he needed a reminder that we were somewhat together. "I hated seeing you sleep with Foss."

I tried to tame the beast within me that was harder to stuff into a box and put away to be dealt with later. I'd been spending far too much time with Foss, because my first instinct was to punch Jens in the throat so he could never say anything so stupid to me again. I waited a few beats before my inner ferocious beast quieted. Then I spoke in our usual whisper. "I hated seeing you getting ridden by two naked women while strung out on Undra heroine, but whatcha gonna do about it? I think I'll make my peace with it."

That shut him up about Foss. "I think your cape is slipping, Supergirl," he chided, moving his face back from mine to better carry his shame.

"Sorry. That wasn't fair."

"No. That's exactly what it was. You just don't usually throw as low as I do."

I turned his chin to angle toward me again. "I can't believe how crazy you must be if you think Foss and I could ever be... I can't even say it. It's gross."

"Never thought I'd see you all cozied up to a half-naked Foss. That was some swift medicine."

"Shut up and kiss me. Logic's starting to take over again."

Jens jumped on his opportunity and pressed his lips to mine, sedating me before I rethought the nature of our fragile relationship.

When he pulled away, a glimmer of clarity flickered in the back of my brain. "We should see other people."

Jens jerked as if I'd slapped him. "What? Are you joking? Was it that bad a kiss?"

"Of course not." I pressed my lips to his once more. "I just don't think I can handle the crushing blow if you cheat on me again. Seeing other people would lower my expectations. Plus, less stress for you while you get over the powder hump. You can be with other girls who can give you what I'm not ready to."

His hands retracted from their home around me as if I was covered in something sticky. "What? Where do you get off making the rules in this?"

I shrugged, unperturbed. "Easy. You're the risk, so I have to calculate the cost. This takes the pressure off."

"Off who? I don't feel any pressure being with you. Are you saying you're feeling pressure from me?" He placed his hands atop his head to keep them honest. "I'm sorry, Loos. I thought you were into every kiss. I've been reading it all wrong. I'm so, so sorry."

I laughed quietly. "No, no." I pecked his lips. "Nothing like that. Every kiss has been exactly what I wanted and needed. I'm talking about pressure for you to stay monogamous. I don't want to put that on you and make you relapse, so if there's no expectation that you're with just me, maybe you'll stay sober longer."

Jens blinked at me, and then moved me off his lap. "I need some air." He went out where the others were, their feet dangling off the ledge as they searched in the sky for oddly-shaped storm clouds, trying not to let the boredom get to them. He looked out onto the water that was still at least two meters deep a mile out. "I curse this stupid place!" he shouted with his fist in the air, making Britta jump. "Curse Bedra and everything in it!" He tugged at his collarbone and ran his hand around his neck, searching for the powder pouch that was not there. "Screw it. I'm going for help."

"Jens, no!" Britta exclaimed, jumping to her feet to stop her brother from climbing over the ledge. She pointed to the sky. "It's not even done raining for good yet. You can't swim that far."

"I probably can." He stretched his back and rubbed a sore spot on his arm to ready it for the task.

"Probably? You're still learning to cope with the pain of your job without the powder! You can't do this!" Then I saw Britta do something she rarely did. Girlfriend stood in front of her brother and yelled. "For once in your life, stop running from your problems! Whatever you're afraid of, go back to your cave and talk it out with Lucy before you throw away the best thing that's ever happened to you!"

Jens was as shocked as I was. He stared at his sister as if

she'd grown a second head. "I'm not running from Lucy. I'm running toward a solution. Anyone else tired of sitting on this mountain?" He raised his hand and started the trend of a couple other hands lifting uncertainly. "That's what I thought."

Britta looked to the back of the cave at my dumbstruck face I tried quickly to compose as I stood. "Lucy, is he running away? Are you two fighting?"

"I don't know," I admitted. "But Jens can go wherever he wants. He doesn't have to stay with me."

Jens turned to me and mimed stabbing himself in the heart with a knife. The hurt on his face was awful to see; he was usually so cool about things. He cleared the distance between us and kissed me just once. "I would have stayed with you till the very end. You only had to ask me."

"I did," I breathed, "and you didn't stay. I know I can't make you be with me."

Jens kissed the scabbed-over cut on my cheek and wound his fingers around my hair, gripping tight to pull me closer. He whispered with pained desperation in my ear, "Damn this caring that we do. It was so much easier before I loved you! Be with whoever you want, but I'm done looking. I'll wait until you know that I'm the only guy for you. You can go through every guy in the phone book. I'll wait till you're sure I won't slip again."

My heart pounded in my chest. I wasn't sure if we were breaking up, or if we were even together enough to warrant a re-breaking up. Or maybe we were floating in that relationship limbo I suggested. Whatever it was, the surface was too far above my head to do or say the right things that would, of course, occur to me moments after. As it was, all I could mutter was a simple, "Okay" before I was left breathless by the unwavering look in his eye. "Don't run from this," I whispered.

"I'm not running." Then he released me, pressed his spine to the back of the cave, took a deep breath and shot himself forward. Jens ran past everyone and leapt off the edge of the cavern, catapulting himself out and freefalling to the waterlogged land below.

I shrieked. I know it was something incoherent, but it was meant to be a "what-are-you-doing-you-idiot" kind of sentiment.

Britta called after him, fearful she would never see her brother again. "Jens! Come back here!"

It was no use. Jens swam away in his perfect breast-stroke toward the buildings in the distance so far away, they could scarcely be seen.

12

DOESN'T SAVE THE DAY

Jens did not come back that night, or the night after that. Britta was certain he had run off to The Den with no intention of coming back. We followed his form until we could not make him out anymore in the darkness. The others turned in that first night, but Britta, Jamie and I stayed awake, searching the black for the most stubborn mule in Bedra.

On the second night when I finally decided to sleep with everyone, I laid down between Foss and Britta, attempting comfort on the rigid rock.

Foss scooted over to make room and murmured, "So you're now driving men to jump off cliffs just to get away from you. Can't say I'm surprised."

"How long you been sitting on that? There're at least four better jabs than what you dug up. I'm insulted your insults are so lame. You're losing your edge," I snapped back. "Shut up and leave me alone. I can't believe I still have to say that to you. You'd think you would have learned by now."

"Learned what? That you cost us the second most valuable member of our team?"

"He's coming back," I argued, biting my lip and shutting my eyes as I willed my words to be true.

"If he doesn't, it's on you," Foss snarled.

"You're the one who made him think we were hooking up!" I whispered.

"You could do worse."

I sat up and pretended to barf in slow motion all over his face and chest as he grinned. "When this is over, I'll be so glad to be rid of you. A world of space between us will be a breath of fresh air."

"When this is over, you'll miss me every day because you'll have no one to fight with." Foss patted the ground next to him. "Lay down, little rat."

"I hate you so much." I stood up and hobbled over near the edge of the alcove, deciding again that I would not sleep with them, but risk falling off a cliff to get a little space.

Waking from slumber brought stiffness I'd only heard old people complain about. Foss was a jerk, but boy, was he a great pillow. I'd never had a proper massage before, but I made a mental note to schedule the longest one ever when this was all over. It was the wind that woke me before the others. I looked up and groaned at the onset of yet more rainclouds. The plains weren't even halfway drained yet, and there was more darkness looming. The weather made my insides feel gloomy, and I began to wonder how long the others would wait for Jens once the water level sank to an acceptable level.

Uncle Rick woke up, but he was the only other one besides me who couldn't sleep. He moved away from the others and sat beside me on the ledge, our feet dangling over just to test our daring.

"Why aren't you sleeping, Goose?" he whispered with his small grandfatherly smile.

"Thanks for asking that like you don't already know. I'm a pathetic mess who waits up for her non-boyfriend to come home. When they asked in kindergarten, I think that was exactly what I said I wanted to be when I grew up."

Alrik chuckled softly. "It's perfectly acceptable to wait up for a member of the team. However, I daresay Jens is a stubborn one. He'll come back when he's ready." When I did not respond, he continued, and I could tell he was choosing his words carefully. "It's no surprise that you ended up with someone who has a stubborn streak to match yours. I wonder which of you will be the first mule to blink."

I wanted to argue on principal, but Uncle Rick had a way of making me see things in the proper light, blinding though the brightness was. "Do you think he's coming back? Or is he knee-deep in The Den, and you're all treating me like a child again by not telling me?"

Uncle Rick took the underhanded correction with grace. "I should have told you. I'm sorry." He straightened next to me and looked out on the water. "But no. I don't think he's slipped back into his habits. Oh, lavender powder is a powerful thing, but so are you. I have faith in our friend." He looked down his hook nose at me. "So should you."

There was something about the wind and the elevation that made it feel like we were the only two people in the world. There was a privacy to it I had not felt in a long time. "Uncle Rick, do you regret bringing me over to your side and signing me up for this mission?"

Alrik's shoulders lowered, and there was a hard look in his gray eyes as he watched the wind tease the water and make small waves. "Every day, though not for the reason you're thinking. I was right in my assumption that you would prove yourself a valuable asset. You destroyed a sea creature that's been besting seasoned sailors for years. You killed a Were and have managed to transition into laplanding with grace. Jamie's curse is almost non-existent now. And of course, you'll be strong and brave enough to tear down the portal when it comes time for that." He pursed his lips before continuing. "But I would take it all back if anyone else could prove to be an asset even half as useful as you. You're older now," he observed, folding his hands in his lap. "I did that to you. It's a crime I hope to pay heavily for once this is all over. You used to sing for no reason. I took that from you. Every scar and bump you endure is my fault, so I regret the decision to put you through this very much. I know you don't understand everything I do, but I do love you, dear. If you understand that, I can die a contented man."

"Love you, too," I echoed, though the words felt hollow. "Why did you pick me? You had the whole of humanity to choose from. Not to state the obvious, but there's a slew of people better suited for this. I just don't buy that I'm the best for the job. Was Vin Diesel really that busy?"

Alrik looked down at his hands and waited a few beats before answering. "I admit I did not check Mr. Diesel's schedule." He sighed, and I could hear his age in the breath. "I needed you close. See, you're valuable to Pesta, so I had to keep you far away from her. If she gets ahold of you, it's all over for the Other Side."

I turned to look at him, wondering what the crap he was talking about. "Huh? I'm human. Pesta shouldn't give two rips about me."

"Yes, but you're purely human when you shouldn't have been. You should have the Huldra whistle or elf elemental magic in you, but you don't. You managed to cling to your humanity."

"So? Why would she care about that? If anything, it makes me less cool."

"Your humanity *is* your magic. Your humanity makes you a danger to Pesta. I would never compromise a weapon so useful. You killed the farlig fisk with nothing but your humanity, my dear." Alrik leaned forward and whispered out onto the water instead of looking at me. "The portals in Undra are made up of specific bones. No one realizes that. They just think the bones in Elvage are random fallen elves Pesta scavenged bones from to make the doorway. But they're not. They're all my relations." He glanced at me to make sure I was paying attention. "Same with Tor's portal and the rest. It's a rare bit of magic, but she's bound it so that you don't just need someone from that race to destroy the portal. All of the portals could have been done simply by Foss and Jens if that were the case. But it has to be someone from that race and that family to break the portal. You and Charles are the only ones who can destroy the human portal, Lucy." He looked down at me with love and sadness. "Were it not for that, I would have sent you to a nunnery when Pesta began targeting you with the Weres."

"Nunnery," I repeated wryly with a snort.

"Indeed. Do you think I wish my favorite niece be exposed to the Nøkkendalig? The Depravity of Man curse? Foss? No. I wish you the very same white picket fence you long for."

I swallowed, taking in his words with equal measures of warmth and a grain of salt. "Targeting me? This whole thing's pretty far to go for just revenge on my mom for stealing her rake."

Uncle Rick folded his hands in his lap. "Pesta knows you're the only threat to cutting her off from her source of human souls. If she kills you, no one can destroy her human portal, and she can actually complete it, thus sticking the human side forever with the Land of Be. How many people do you know who can actually afford a retirement? The Land of Be would change a lot of things for your world. A society crumbles without its elders."

"What about Charles? He's a threat to her, then, right?"

Alrik nodded. "He is, but like most of Undra, she undervalues him. Besides, no one knows of his human lineage, other than our group." He glanced behind at his surrogate son. "In Undra, when you adopt someone, they become part of your family legally, of course, but they also become your blood relation."

I paused, letting that settle to see if it made any sense. "You mean figuratively?"

"No. Your blood actually changes, your basic genetics. You still have bits of your birth parents, but you also have an added gene in there from your adoptive parents. It's a very old magic."

My eyes widened. "Whoa! That's awesome. Totally poetic. So Charles is half mine and half yours?"

Uncle Rick chuckled. "Oh, Goosy. Now that he's met you? He'll always be yours. But yes, his blood is your mother's, father's, and a little of mine. It's why he can do two kinds of elf magic, and could be called on to destroy the elfish portal and the human one, if need be." He scratched his nose, refusing to glance over at me. "I want you to look after him when this is all over."

"Might be kinda hard to do. I'll be in my world.

Fun as Undra is with its views on women and the constant danger of it all, I belong with proper plumbing."

Alrik smiled, but the levity faded. "However you can manage it. Come and visit him regularly or let him stay with you on your side. Whatever works for you both. Just please don't leave him without family."

I squinted up at my uncle. "Well, he'll have you, too, but that's fine. I wasn't planning on never seeing him again after this. He can stay with me as long as he wants. You know I'd never ditch my family." I twiddled my thumbs as I tried to find a tactful way of stating my concerns. "He called me 'baby'."

With a sage expression that suited his high level of knowledge, Alrik kept his voice low. "Yes. He's not used to pretty girls paying him any mind, and he's never had a sister. Certainly not one like you. He was bound to get confused."

I wanted to give a goofy grin at the compliment, but life was just too complicated for that right now. "So long as he can get our roles straight, he can come visit me any old time."

Alrik lowered his voice further, and I had to really listen close to hear him over the wind. "I want you to take Foss with you to the Other Side and keep him there after the mission's over."

My face mutated into a contorted grimace, as if I'd just eaten a lemon. Foss often left me with that feeling. "Um, no thanks. Sure, he'll come for the mission, but then he's going back to Undra."

"Where in Undra is Foss safe? He's well-known, and he's supposed to be dead. If the wrong person recognizes him, he'll be hunted by Olaf until he's actually killed this time."

I wanted to be flippant about that, but I tried to be an adult. "That sounds like a problem for Undra or your diplomatic genius to figure out. You know he won't fit in my world. He'll up and get himself shot as soon as he opens his sexist mouth. We'll be lucky if he makes it through the mission over there without causing too much a stir."

Alrik nodded. "He'll have a lot of changing to do, that's for certain. He doesn't have other options, though. Charles is working on stripping the curse from him, and I daresay I've noticed a change. I have faith he can grow. I also have faith you're the one to help him, too. He cares about you."

I scoffed, unable to feign maturity any longer. "If that's him caring, I'll pass." I scowled at my uncle, and instantly felt ashamed for it.

"Lucy, he needs to start over. He needs a guide. You saved his life. Now you're responsible for him."

I stiffened and tried to remember to whisper. "Huh? Where do you get off with that logic?" I shook my head to stave off his answer. "You should love me better than to ask me to watch out for a man who's smacked me around. He's talked down to me and Britta this whole trip, and you've all just let him. Don't think I don't notice you not defending me when he gets too rough." I avoided his hurt gaze and looked out over the drowned plains. "Curse or not, if you actually loved me, you wouldn't let him be that way around me. No way would my dad've stood for it. I wish I could count on you. I've always wished it." I sniffed, tugging my hair back from my face as the wind picked up. "When my family died, you came for like, a weekend and left. You talk a good game about loving us and all that, but you left me to fend for myself after all my blood up and died. Now you let Foss knock me around and talk to me like I'm garbage. Your love hasn't saved the day in a long time." I brought a knee to my chest. "And what kind of love doesn't save the day?"

Uncle Rick let silence rest between us while the breeze picked up with an edge of chill to it. "As much as I wanted to ensure you could carry on after they died, I knew you would. I've always known you were a survivor. And Lucy," he looked out into the gray sky with a closed expression, "Charles is my responsibility and my son. He lost his mother and father, too. Only unlike you, he doesn't have a plethora of happy memories to pool from. His hope that one day they might come back for him was dashed forever." Alrik picked at a thread on his sleeve. "Charles did not handle the deaths well. That you are here now, well, it's done more healing than anything I did while abandoning you ever accomplished."

I looked over my shoulder at my sleeping brother. His

long black hair was greasy and messy. He lay on his back with his hand over his belly. "I guess I never thought about Charles in all of it."

"No one ever does." Alrik scratched his beard as he thought. "Though, I am sorry. For everything, really. I've been a terrible uncle to you. When Pesta murdered your parents, it was the last straw. I've been consumed ever since." He rubbed a hand down his face and rested it on his jaw as he sighed. The sound was weary, like he'd lived far longer than his allotted time. "It's almost done. Two more portals, and she's cut off."

My voice was quieter than the whisper, and Alrik had to lean in to hear me. "Pesta built the portals, though. Won't she just build more? I mean, is what we're doing going to stick?"

"That's for me to worry about." Alrik placed his hand on my shoulder. "And I wouldn't be concerned about Foss. He'll learn."

"If you say so." I squinted at the cloud overhead that looked like it might burst at any moment. "It's our friendly neighborhood storm cloud again. This weather is nuts."

Alrik and I moved back into the cave just as the sky opened on us again. There was four seconds of preamble before the floodgates opened. There was not a whole lot of room, so I leaned against the wall while the others slept and Alrik laid down next to Foss.

"Lucy," Charles whispered, lifting his head, but not the rest of his body.

For no reason other than being an overly emotional girl in that moment, my heart ached for Mace's plight. To pine for the family he would never have, and then get stuck with me in my fractured state. Despite how much he could have hated me for being the one my parents stuck around for, he did not. He'd been nothing short of awesome to me the entire time. I crawled over to him and slid my body between his and Jamie's, wrapping my arms around Mace's neck and hugging him tight.

It was hard to have a private moment when we were all shoved together like sardines, but I managed. I whispered as I held his neck, "I'm sorry our mom and dad died. I'm sorry you never got to meet Linus. I'm sorry it all went down the way it did. If I would've known about you, no way they would've pulled the nonsense they did. Linus and I would've kidnapped you and taken you out of Undraland to live with us. He could've used a big brother like you."

Charles was only just barely awake, but I could see the surprise in his tired eyes. We faced each other and held on as the rain fell, washing away the... just washing it all away.

13

THE NEW RULES

I roused when I felt lips grace my cheek. I was snuggled up to Charles, and Jamie's side was warming my back as the wind howled. I assumed it was one of them being sweet. I swear, after all this was over, I wouldn't miss sleeping on the hard ground, but I would miss the warmth in my soul that came from sleeping between two awesome men.

Water dripped on my face and neck, running down and making me uncomfortable. We were far enough back in the small cave that getting rained on only happened when the wind blew the precipitation sideways, which it was not. I opened my eyes and was greeted by a sight that made my heart ache.

"Is it really you?" I whispered, not wanting to wake the others.

Jens tossed me a crooked smile. He was soaking wet,

but looked pleased with himself as he knelt by my head. "No. It's not me. It's the Australian Outback version of Jens." He switched his whispered cadence to a caricature of an Aussie. "Crikey! It's a slammin' Sheila out in the wild! I wonder if she'll let me take her down unda in my cool boat." Then for good measure, he threw in a confident, "Let's throw another shrimp on the barbie!"

Jamie reached his hand up to slap Jens's. "I knew you'd come back."

Jens stood and clapped his hands together, letting his voice carry so it could not be ignored. "Wake up, kids. Clean and sober Daddy bought you all a shiny new boat. I can take three of you at a time." He helped Jamie and Britta up, hugging his sister and kissing the top of her head. "Sisters first," he declared. "Nothing but the royal treatment for all sisters!"

Britta yawned. "What are you talking about?"

"I swam to moderately dry land. Well, everything's wet and spongy, but there are parts you can walk on. Even parts you can go to haggle for a small boat. Anyone else ready to get off this rock?" The noises of assent were tired, but sincere. "Then let's go. Britt? Alrik? Charles? Grab your gear and climb down. It's slick, but if you're careful you can make it. I'll paddle you ashore, and come back for the next batch of stowaways. I found an abandoned hut we can crash in until the rain stops. Much better than a cave."

He tossed a few apples to the fellow travelers. Charles bit into a green one and groaned. "I was starting to forget what any food other than biscuits tasted like." My brother handed me his apple and stole a bite of the one I'd snatched. Purple. A purple apple. I mean, I had to take it to see what it tasted like. When else would I get to eat a lilac purple apple?

Turns out, purple apples taste the same as a Red Delicious, only spongier. *Barf.* I must've made a face, because Mace consumed the rest of my purple one and left me with his crisp green one. When I could not conceal the admiration for him from my face, I breathed, "You love me."

Charles cocked his head sideways to size up my level of awareness. "That just now dawned on you? I give you my apple, and all of a sudden you understand how much I love you?"

I nodded, holding the green fruit he'd sacrificed so I could have one extra smile. "You gave me the good apple, and I didn't even tell you I wanted it. You love me," I repeated.

"Indeed, I do." He grinned at me, pressing a kiss to my forehead. "You'd better get started on that one, because I'm coming for it next."

I took a meaty, covetous bite, letting the juices run down my chin. It had been a few days since I'd eaten something that didn't leave my mouth like the Sahara. "I love you, too, big brother."

Charles, Alrik and Britta were packed and ready in exactly one minute. Everyone was antsy to get off the mountain and on with the rest of the journey; we didn't even care that our travels would be in the rain.

Jens held my face in his hands and backed me toward our little hideaway in the far end of the cave. Before he said his piece that made his dark eyebrows knit together so intensely, he kissed me. I was still chewing the last of my apple, and his deft tongue stole the bite from me. He pulled back and chewed, making me blanch. "Gross. Too weird," I commented, my fingers tangling in the short hairs at the base of his neck. The thick hair on top of his head was messy, as usual, but the rain made it gather in grabbable clumps.

His arms wrapped around my waist, and he leaned down to whisper in my ear, "You can pretend you want to see other people, but I'm the only one you'd let eat an apple straight from your mouth." He paused for my laugh, then pulled me closer so our wet bodies were pressed together. "I will make this up to you. I *will* make you trust me again." He kissed my lips before I could reply. "We'll get it back. I'll do whatever it takes."

I nodded slowly, not wanting to fight, but also not willing to give in just yet. "I'm still pretty firm on seeing other people, Jens. Solid as your word is, I can't trust you."

He nodded, leaning his forehead to mine. His eyes were scrunched shut to fend off the pain my words inflicted on him. "That's fair. Can I ask you a favor, though?" When I didn't stop him, he whispered. "Don't hook up with Foss, and for sure not Jamie. I couldn't take it."

"How about any other guy in the world? Who would you be able to picture me with?" His forlorn expression changed my tone. "Of course I wouldn't be with your best friend and Britt's fiancé. I'm not trying to hurt you. I just can't expect you to be with only me. I don't have anyone in mind I'm jonesing to hook up with." I considered this, and amended my statement. "Except maybe Tony Danza circa *Who's the Boss*. All bets are off with him."

With his forehead pressed to mine, his words came out only an inch from my lips. "Don't shtick. Not right now. Please don't be with Foss. I notice you left him out of your little song that's killing me softly."

I kissed Jens's soft mouth in a gentle rhythm that made me appreciate how full his lips were. I could hear the others milling around and conversing excitedly about finally getting off the rock. "I didn't mention Foss because that's a ridiculous thing to ask me." How I wished we were not in this murky place. "And you don't have the right to tell me who you can stomach me dating. I didn't get a say when you cheated on me with the naked women who fed on your essence. I would've chosen a toothless hunchback for you to make your move on."

Jens fingered the ring around my neck. "Do what you want, but I'm with you. The lavender powder's why I was in The Den. After that, the Mare pretty much do what they want with you, and I was too smashed to care."

"You're making this so much better. Really."

"Point is, I didn't cheat because I wanted anyone else. I cheated because I was too out of my mind to push them away when they took my clothes off."

My heart ached for simpler days. For a pillow and hot chocolate and a good crap TV show to lose myself in. "You have to know I deserve better than that."

"I know," Jens whispered. "It's just… you're married to Foss and laplanded to my best friend. Your brother's in love with you. I felt like you were slipping through my fingers when I was with you, and I'm still terrified of that."

I kissed him again, sighing with utter contentment that anything felt familiar in this strange place – and that it was him. "I don't want to fight. If we're supposed to be together, we'll figure it out eventually. Everyone's waiting for Superman to fly us off this rock, so take off your glasses, Clark."

I'm not sure what I expected him to do or say, but I for sure was not anticipating the make-out session that came. Jens pressed me against the cave's wall in our private little nook with his hard body, one hand tangling in my hair, and the other sweeping down the slope of my side. I gasped against his mouth when his hand roamed under my shirt and traced my lowest rib. He'd never gone there before. There were a thousand conflicting feelings racing through me, trilling up and down my spine like a minia-ture drag-racer in my nervous system. His kiss was earnest, pleading with me to forget what he'd done, to start over as if this were our first kiss.

I wanted to. Oh, how I wanted to go back to the only simple thing in this world of oddities and complexities. How I wished it could be mine, that he could be mine.

That I could be mine.

"Wait!" I begged. "Wait, stop." We pulled away in the cramped space, catching our breath with our foreheads mashed together. "Don't do that."

"I'm sorry. I got carried away." He shoved his hands in his pockets to keep them honest and mustered an apologetic smile. "I get it. You, upper hand. Me, doghouse. I'm sorry."

"No. We're equals, Jens. The kiss. Don't kiss me to change my mind, to change me. Kiss me because you love me. That's the only reason I ever want a kiss from you."

Jens evaluated my response and nodded slowly. "You're right. That was low. You can feel however you want about us." Then with purposeful hands, he lightly touched my jaw, tipping my face up to his. "I love you, Lucy Kincaid. Only you. It's only ever been you."

Then he kissed me the right way. Slow, meaningful and full of all the things I loved best about him. I could feel his adoration in each movement, his devotion in every hitched breath.

The kiss remained unhurried, but with each measured movement, the emotion ran deeper, like roots wrapping around my heart and tugging me closer to him. I could feel his love for my family, the lengths he had gone to in order to keep us safe. I could taste the heartbreak he suffered when Linus died, and the shock and devastation when my parents followed soon after. When his fingertips traced my face as if it was made of glass, I began to understand the lengths he was willing to go to for us to stay together. His self-loathing over his addiction to the powder was evident, but his determination to put that chapter of his life behind him also rang out as his lips dragged to my cheek and placed a single, lingering kiss there that communicated his permanent place in my life. I was his golden choice, and not his duty that was etched into his golden face tattoo.

Suffice to say, I'd never been kissed like that. The crushing and elating sensations coursed through me, making my scalp tingle and my toes curl. I wanted to say something sophisticated or sexy, but all that came out was a gust of, "What the crap was that?"

Jens smiled through the composure that was escaping him as he breathed against my cheek. "That's our new first kiss." He pressed his stubble to my face and gently nuzzled me. "Every time you start to forget us, let me kiss you like that. I'm here. Beneath the scar, right over your heart." He tapped my heart, and my knees fought for control over the gravity that pulled at me. "I'm always here."

14

SLEIPNIR

Jens and I were attached at a physical and emotional level until the need for physical separation could not be put off any longer. He went down into the boat first and guided the bodies Foss lowered over the edge down into the quaint vessel, ignoring the smattering of rain. It barely held the four, but somehow it worked. The stricken puppy expression tugged at my heart when he begged me with his eyes to be safe until he came back for me. I watched Jens paddle Britta, Alrik and Charles away with slashes of raw emotion on my face.

He came back. No bloodshot eyes, no stink of The Den. Jens rescued me. There were still parts of him worth trusting, so I decided to cling to those for the moment.

Foss whistled. "So, you forgave him?"

Being brought back to the present was like being

yanked down from the clouds down to, well, a cave in the middle of the rain. I shrugged. "Jury's still out. Not ready to throw in the towel just yet."

"Throw in the towel?"

I was grateful Charles kept up Foss's dose of whistled Prozac before he left. Foss was much less likely to get thrown off the mountain by me, or me by him, come to think of it. I waved off the question. "It's a sports term. I'm not ready to give up yet, is what it means."

We watched them row away to a point that could barely be seen through the rain, which was coming down in a heavy drool now. I checked in with Jamie through our bond, since he was unusually quiet. He alternated between worrying for Britta's safety and observing the peppery bunch of tiny gray clouds not too far off.

Jamie scratched his head. "I can feel you doing that, you know."

"What?" I looked around and realized he was talking about me. "How?"

"It starts to feel crowded in my head. Not like you're banging on the door, but like you're right outside it listening for me or something."

"Yikes. Sorry. I was just making sure you were okay."

The cold rain fell just a foot in front of us, providing a semi-transparent curtain that separated us from the whole of Undra. Jamie reached out for my hand in a move uncharacteristic of the proper man. I migrated to his side, feeling the little sister to the giant, hulking big brother. "If I told you to hide in that little nook you love to share with Jens, would you listen to me?"

My alerts went up, and I squeezed his hand. "Of course. What's going on?"

He squinted into the sky at the gray blobs that were moving quicker than the clouds around them. "Do you have Sleipnir on the Other Side?"

"Huh? The eight-legged horse things? No."

Foss stiffened and pulled his sword out of his bag. "Sleipnir can't fly this great a distance. The flood's too vast. It's not possible, Jamie."

Jamie followed me into my little hiding spot on the right side of the cave toward the back, and then kissed the top of my head. "Stay put, *liten syster*." He pulled out a short dagger from his pack and closed my fingers around it, his serious expression trying to force out calm for me. "In case we fall." His hand gripped over mine and gave a few practice jabs to an imaginary foe. "Aim to kill. In and up before you retract." He jerked my hand forward and dragged it up, gutting the imaginary beast. "In and up."

My eyes were wide, and I suddenly forgot how to breathe. Yet Jamie was composed as he spoke of whatever doom was bearing down on us. "What, Jamie? What's going on?"

He pressed the fist holding the dagger to my chest. "Keep yourself hidden, now. Don't come out until I tell you it's safe." Then he turned invisible.

My skin was instantly cold and wet with sweat. Anxiety

flooded my veins as if coming into me from an amphetamine IV drip I was tethered to. I obeyed with clumsy feet, casting a look of concern at Foss. He gave me a solitary nod as a means of conveying some unspeakable connection he would never admit he felt toward me.

I plastered my body tight to the furthest corner of my little make-out space, wishing we had all found a way to escape aboard the dinghy together.

Foss backed himself into me, the muscles in his shoulders tight with a soldier's intuition. He tied a rope around one of the boulders and tossed the end to Jamie, who took up his post on the other side of the cave. He tied it around a similar rock and tossed it back to Foss. They repeated the motion until they had made a web of sorts, closing us on the side separate from the rain that was starting to pick up.

Foss turned to face me, pressing his overlarge body as far into the narrow alcove as possible. There was scarcely room for my lungs to expand as he smeared me to the wall with his naked chest. The overpowering thrum of claustrophobia banged around in my body, but I fought to control myself. "Foss, what…"

His hand covered my mouth, and he shook his head. "How do the Weres always find you?" It wasn't exactly an accusation, but it wasn't a straight question, either. "It's you. No matter where we go, Pesta's tracking you. Why? How?" If he expected an answer, he did not wait for it. He pushed the dagger flat against my chest. "Stay hidden. If it's you she wants, we won't give you to her." He paused his thought to press a closed-mouth kiss to my lips. My stomach was already in knots, but it managed to do a backflip in its befuddled state. "If it comes to you to fight, show no mercy."

I could hear the rain and the blood rushing in my ears. Then I heard a whooshing outside the cave that matched my pounding heart. Foss was pushed up against me, holding his breath as something hard like hooves clomped on the floor of the cave. I counted three beasts by my hearing, though I could not see them to confirm what sort they were. I thought invisible thoughts, willing my body to melt into the rock. I'd read about monks who had mastered the whole mind-over-matter thing, but knew I was not on their level of awesomeness.

Snorting and a sort of breathy growling came from the creatures, adding to my already overactive imagination. They gnawed at the ropes and I heard hacking.

Then it started.

I heard Jamie lunge to the middle of the cave, slashing with his sword. High-pitched screeching that sounded like metal ripping rang in my ears. Foss tore himself from our hiding spot and came out with his blade swinging. His exclamations of surprise frightened me, and I heard a mix of metal and animal fighting for the limited ground.

"There's too many!" Jamie shouted. "Don't let them corner you!"

My hand shook as it gripped the dagger that felt simultaneously too heavy to lift and too small to be of use. I heard flesh tearing and more of the enemy's screams. Then I felt a swift kick to my chest, and the air knocked out of me. I did not cry out, but my ribs burned as I fought for breath. I fished around in Jamie's head to get a look at what bested him so easily.

My jaw dropped as the image of several enormous winged horses came into my consciousness. They were gray, larger than life, flying, and I counted eight spidery legs on each one. The horses were foaming at the mouth and had yellow eyes that made their matted gray coat that much more dead looking. On the hooves, I noticed not horseshoes, but claw-like talons, painted with fresh and dried blood.

Most shocking of all were the riders. Each of the five Sleipnir was ridden by a man just as rabid and deranged as its animal. Yellow eyes searched manically for something they could not see. Saliva and foam coated their chins, and their speech was distorted as they fought.

"Don't kill the riders!" Jamie insisted. "They're possessed!"

One of the mutant horses reared up and bucked at Foss, who shoved his body into our nook. His shoulder was bleeding, but he seemed more ticked off than injured. He growled as he lunged out again, gutting and tearing with both blade and bare hands. He fought off one that was coming for Jamie as the prince wrestled his own Sleipnir. They switched places, and Jamie was closer to me now, his horse and rider baring down on him as Foss found himself in another fight he could not barrel his way out of.

The horse stomped down, hoping to crush the invisible man, but Jamie was quick. He rolled yet closer to me, but the horse was no fool. The rider had Jamie cornered.

There was no time for a moral debate. There was no room for hesitation. I climbed up using the sides of the tight walls and angled my head around so I could see the snout of the horse. Without waiting for a better idea to pop into my head, my arm shot around the bend just as Jamie's sword plunged upward. I screamed as my dagger sunk deep into the horse's eye socket. I wrenched it out as it bucked backwards and fell off the side of the mountain.

Suddenly my world spun. I was no longer in the nook. I was on the floor of the cave, looking up at... me.

15

ZOMBIES ON METH

nother Sleipnir replaced the one Jamie and I had killed together, giving me no time to evaluate the situation. I scarcely had time to look down at my new invisible body before a rider dismounted and came at me like a zombie on meth. I took the sword that Jamie had been holding and rammed it into the chest of the man, sobbing an apology as I retracted the weapon and kicked him over the ledge with a boot that was not mine.

Then the strangest thing happened. My body flew out from the nook, and from the back of the cave, I saw myself fighting with a Sleipnir on the ledge.

I gripped Jamie's sword as my brain caught up. Jamie and I laplanded again by killing that horse together. Instead of tying us together, it switched our bodies. My hands were strong and manly, and my body was tall and capable. Jamie had caught on, and was using my body to fight with trained vigor I had never before possessed.

"Lucy, get back!" Foss shouted as he threw a rider off his horse.

But my body didn't listen. Jamie leaped off the edge of the cave and clawed his way onto the back of the Sleipnir whose rider had been upended, and was currently swimming below. I watched Jamie use my body to slice across the horse-spider's throat with the dagger I'd been given in case of emergency.

I screamed a low-pitched but still girly utterance that made Foss turn his head in the heat of battle as a rider dismounted and charged at me with a chain and mace swinging.

In that moment, I found my footing. Shedding my invisibility like flipping a switch, I stood and brought my sword down hard at an angle on the meth zombie's neck. It wasn't the most expert of slices, but it delivered a decent cut that would give him a slow bleed out. "I'm sorry!" I yelled, stepping back as he took a determined, but drunken step toward me. "Don't make me do this!"

He responded with a garbled version of "screw you" or something to that effect. Despite the handicap, he lifted the chain and flicked his wrist to fling the mace straight for my head. I ducked, but operating Jamie's body felt a little like running a construction crane while wearing a mattress. Everything was too tall, too beefy. I felt the mace swipe across my now curly brown hair and let out a choked squeal as I hunched in a ball.

The mace was coming again, so I resorted to my limited knowledge of gymnastics and did a somersault, knocking into the meth zombie's legs and bumping him from his already janky stance. In his stumble, I yanked the chain from him. My body was so big; it was easy to see Jamie doing the things I did. Jamie would have no problem wrapping the chain around the zombie's neck. He would not hesitate to tighten the noose and choke out the once-human. I sobbed as I felt the life drain from the undead man. I trembled as I tightened the noose beyond what was necessary just to make sure the job was done.

As yet another spider horse landed on the precipice, something in me shifted. I was no longer Lucy the Pacifist. I became Jamie the Destroyer. I punched the horse in the throat, and watched as Foss ran it through with his sword. I jumped back as it reared on its hind four legs, bucking out at me beyond what I was able to dodge quick enough. One of its talon hooves scraped me down the outside of my arm, and I shrieked in pain. I glanced up at my body that was still choking out the Sleipnir midair. Jamie did not flinch at the pain or the blood that streaked down our arms. He remained focused on the task at hand. With teeth gritted and muscles shaking, Jamie stayed focused on his task of taking out the threat. I had never seen myself look so determined or more heroic.

Tears streaked my Jamie face, and I watched as my body stabbed the flying spider horse, and then leaped from it just as it lost its flight and plummeted into the water below. I pulled my body up with far more ease than should be natural. I had no idea Jamie was so strong. I towered over me, and finally realized how fragile I looked to them.

Foss kicked the last Sleipnir over the side and knocked out the final bad guy with three swift blows to the temple. "What is this?" he demanded of me. "How is Pesta possessing *people*? They look like my kin!" He examined the unconscious man's dark-skinned face as his chest heaved, coming down from the fight with every breath.

I looked out over the water and saw Jens rowing toward us with such tenacity, it looked as if he might leap from the canoe if it would get him to us sooner. "It's Jens!" I said, standing on my toes and waving him down. I turned back to Foss and gasped at the gash across his chest and the deep cut at his shoulder. "Oh, Foss! Let me look at that. Don't worry. I'm sure I can fix it." I gently fluttered my fingers across a scrape on his forehead.

I must've looked like a giant girl, because despite the craze of battle, Foss looked at me like I was the most confusing bug he'd ever seen. He backed away, regarding me without his usual coat of hatred or irritation. "I'm fine, Jamie."

Oh, right. I'm Freaky Friday'd with my laplanding buddy. "I'm not Jamie," I clarified, pointing to my body. I glanced over and watched myself look down curiously and grab my breasts. "Hey!" I barked. "Hands off! Those are mine, Jamie. Be cool."

Jamie unhanded my breasts in shock, as if only just realizing what he was doing. Both our faces turned red as he stammered an apology. "I wasn't thinking. Forgive me, Lucy." He set about examining his various cuts and gouges, unable to look me in the eye.

Foss's head whipped from Jamie to me and back again until the shocking information sunk in. "You... how? Jamie, what?"

Jamie explained the double laplanding and the unforeseen consequences, leaving Foss at a loss for words. Jens finally reached us, and Jamie was the only one with his wits about him enough to warn Jens about the dead bodies directly below us so his canoe did not get stuck on them.

Foss was somber as he lowered my body down into the canoe. I watched with equal amounts of amusement and horror as Jens wrapped his arms around my body and kissed my lips.

Jamie squirmed and wormed his way out of Jens's grip, leaving my poor boyfriend with a stricken expression. I listened to the condensed version of things again and watched Jens go pale. When we were all in the boat, including the hogtied unconscious man, Jens had a hard time looking at us. Every time he glanced at either Jamie or me, he squinted and turned his head back to the paddle, as if we were the sun that was too bright for his eyes.

Judging by his grim expression, I voiced my biggest fear of the moment. "Is it permanent, then?"

Jens offered up an unconvincing smile. "No. I'm sure it's not. We'll find a way to get you back, babe... Lucy." He grimaced as we made eye contact and turned away again. Jamie put a small hand on my back, and I could see the doom dawning on him, as well.

16

FREAKY FRIDAY

Britta tried to kiss me, but she was easy to fend off and rattle off the story to. Her response was different than Jens's. He responded by avoiding both of us, lest he accidentally kiss either his best friend's body or his being. Britta sat between us, holding both our hands to offer whatever comfort she could. When it comes to being awesome, women really have a leg up in these kinds of circumstances. You know, the times where you switch bodies with your best girlfriend's boyfriend.

Jens and Alrik were deep in planning mode to rectify the situation as quick as possible. Foss had wrestled the possessed man Pesta used to attack us to a chair in the dank hut, tying him securely to the wood. We were inside a small house on a hill that Jens had scouted out for us. The owners could not get to their home because of the surrounding flood, so we squatted to get some rest from the rain.

Foss changed into dry clothes like the others had done, but Jamie and I sat in our soaking clothing, too respectful of the other person's body to disrobe. Thank God for Jamie. If it'd been some perv I double laplanded with, I'd be pretty batty right about now.

Jens gave up on the powwow and sat next to me, leaning against the wall with a grim expression. "We don't know how to undo it," he admitted.

I drew my new knees up to my chest and tried not to break down in girlish tears. I nodded, gulping back any hope that had managed to fight to see the light of day. "Okay." My giant hands could do serious damage, but they held no comfort for me anymore. Little marks and quirks on my female body tugged at my heart as I began to say goodbye to them. For all the insecure moments where I sucked in my tummy or was disappointed by my reflection, I realized I didn't hate my body after all. I should have made fewer foolish decisions. I should have been kinder to it. I should have been kinder to myself.

I jerked my chin to the door. "Looks like you're off the hook. You can go back to your Den and do what you want now." I managed a weak smile that broke my heart as I tried to force bravery and the high road upon myself. "No hard feelings. We had a good go of it."

Jens softened, wrapping an arm around my hairy back. "Lucy," he crooned in my ear.

It was too much. The damn broke and the tears poured out of me. Jens was the one thing that was mine. Now he was the home I would never get to keep. It was better being able to say a decent goodbye, but feeling his arms around my giant body, I knew there would be little light without his constant glow for me.

Jens gripped my shoulder. "I don't know where you got it in your head that I just like you for your smokin' body. Sure, this one'll take some getting used to, but you're still you." He gave my cheek a light slap so I would turn my head and meet his determined gaze. "I love you, and I'm not going anywhere."

I rolled my eyes. "Right. The tattoo. You're promised to my family." I balled up my fists and dug them into my cheeks, feeling the short beard there. "Ugh! What a sucky life for you! You're stuck with me."

Jens pulled my hands from my face and nuzzled my nose with his. "Baby, I'm not stuck. I want to be with you."

"No, you don't. Not like you did before. I can see it. You look at me different. Why wouldn't you?"

Jens laughed. "Well, for one, you have a beard now. It's going to take more than a couple hours to get used to. And sure, I don't know how all the details are going to work out, but it's not like we were having sex before. We're still getting to know each other, taking it slow. We'll keep doing that."

He held my face, and I had to close my eyes to fend off the love radiating from him. It was too big, too accepting of the freak show I had yet to make peace with. "I'm sorry. I didn't mean to double-lapland with your best friend. I understand if you want to call it quits."

"Shh." Jens leaned in and closed the breath of a gap between us, pressing his lips to mine.

My heart spluttered and parts of me reacted very differently than I was prepared for. The room went silent, save for the thrashing man in the center Foss had tied to a chair. Jens's lips were still soft as our facial hair bristled and brushed. When my eyes finally opened, I could see his devotion to me – his utter refusal to let us part. No matter what, it seemed we were in this until the end.

Jamie was horrified to watch a romantic kiss between himself and his best friend. "Ah! I don't want to see that!"

Jens raised his arms in the air in triumph. "Yes! I win! That's it. You're marrying me. It's done. It's decided."

He looked so proud of himself, I couldn't help but laugh. "How'd you work that out?"

"Because I loved you even when you were a man. What other guy's gonna say that? It's over. Anyone else is a distant second. No more of this open relationship garbage. We're sealed. It's done."

I could not erase my smile. Only Jens would know how to turn this horror into a joke, and somehow get me to laugh along with him. "How do I know this wasn't your plan all along? Pretty convenient, this flood. You just *had* to go leave us in your canoe so Jamie and I would of course switch bodies. You've had your eye on this prize for years, but Jamie would never go for it." I rubbed my man chest seductively.

"I usually get what I want," Jens replied, holding onto my hand. The levity turned to tenderness with a single look from his beautiful eyes. "We'll figure it out, Loos. So long as you're you, I'll follow you to the ends of Undraland, and then to the Other Side."

Foss broke up the sweet moment, as that was his nature. "Could we move on from the most disturbing sight I've ever seen?" His fist yanked on the rabid man's ponytail, jerking his head up so it did not thrash around so violently. "I need to know how Pesta keeps finding us, and this is the first time we might be able to get some answers."

The man gnashed his teeth at me. There was no mistaking that either Jamie or I was his intended target.

Alrik gave me a grave look that made my spine stiffen. "I think you and Britta might prefer the rain to the business we're going to conduct in a moment, Lucy dear."

"What business?" Then I saw Foss cracking his knuckles and Jens standing to sharpen his knife on a stone he'd brought inside, both looking with a cold calculation at the rabid man. "Oh, torture? Yeah, I don't want to be here for that. Is it really necessary? I mean, he's a real live person beneath what Pesta did to him. I'm guessing he can't give you information, even if he wanted to cooperate. She's controlling him."

"That may be, but we're running out of options." Alrik placed his hand on Foss's shoulder. "Wait until Lucy leaves the house. She doesn't need this to keep her up at night. She's already seen too much as it is."

"I'll stay," Britta ruled.

"You coddle your niece, Alrik," Foss argued, glaring at my body. I watched Jamie stand and try to meet Foss's intimidation with his own, but my petite stature compared to Foss's let a little air out of the tires. "Sit down, woman," he sneered at Jamie.

Jamie did not hold to my pacifist views. His fists clenched as he stepped forward and shoved Foss, clearly having hit his limit with all things frustrating when he lost his penis.

Foss responded as Foss was trained to. He backhanded my body and sent me flying down to the floor.

Jens and Charles immediately got in Foss's face while Alrik helped Jamie up. "You can't treat her like that!" Jens growled.

Foss's nose scrunched as he glanced from me to Jamie. "Well, what are the rules now? This is confusing."

"How about no one hits anybody? Novel concept," I jabbed, wishing I didn't live in a world where I had to say things like that. I rubbed my sore cheek and glared at Foss, who really should've known better by now.

Jamie sat back down next to Britta, who fretted over him. I could see the irritation building in him at being babied, but he was too well-mannered to rebuke Britta.

I intervened. "Come on, Jamie. Let's go outside. I need to talk to you."

When we got outside, both of us breathed a little easier, even though it was rainy and wet. Jamie let out a grunt of frustration as he leaned against the house in my soaking clothes. "I hate this!" he bellowed. The way he carried my body was different. He was used to a wider gait, and he crossed his arms a lot more. It was mildly entertaining to watch myself be... different.

"I know. So let's fix it."

"Do you think I want to watch me make out with my best friend?" He snorted at me. "No one can fix laplanding. It's a law of nature. You can't undo it. You have no idea the permanence of these things."

I turned away from him and looked out at the flood. Miles and miles of water separated us from the place we killed that stupid possessed Sleipnir that got us in this pickle in the first place. "Don't talk to me like I'm an idiot. When the others do it, I get it, but you're in my head. You should know how that hurts me."

Jamie hung my head and centered himself. "You're right. That wasn't fair."

"I'm not naïve. But I'm also not a quitter. Have you ever heard of something like this happening?"

"Never." Jamie banged the back of my head against the wall in frustration.

"Then we don't know it can't be undone. Let's think about the problem logically for a second before going off the deep end into the pit of despair. My gosh, you Undra people are so dramatic." I looked down at my hairy knuckles and smiled. "Not that there aren't perks to being you. I'm so tall, and people look at me like I can do anything. It's like this body came with built-in respect. Kinda awesome."

"Well, I hate being you. They look at me like I'm five years old. They talk over me, as if I have nothing of value to say. Like I can't help or do anything for myself. And Foss? He never would have dared strike me before this."

I took his harsh assessment of my body in stride. "Sucks, doesn't it. But you didn't hear me whining, and Foss has done worse than backhand me, chief. I know who I am, and so should you. Deal or whine. I don't care which, just do it quietly. I'm trying to think."

It was then that the torture started. Bile rose in my throat at the sound, and my mind raced to find a solution to all the problems of the day.

I focused on my short, filthy fingernails, wishing there was some way to dig out the dirt that looked permanent. I wondered if Charles had a whistle that could control grime.

I lifted Jamie's head slowly as pieces of the puzzle moved closer to fitting together if I jammed them in just the right way. Mouth dropped open, I raised my head to the sky and caught the first glimpse of sunlight breaking through the relentless rain clouds. "Jamie, I've got it!"

17

SOULS AND BODIES

"Stop! Stop it, Jens! Wait!" I cried as I burst through the door.

Jens retracted the dagger he had stuck in the man's arm and hid it, ashamed he was caught in the act of being barbaric. "Lucy, go outside." Despite his bravado-laced kiss, Jens still had a hard time looking at me. He grimaced when he said my name.

"Don't hurt him. I've got an idea."

"Now's not the time for your stupid chatter, Lucy." At least Foss was predictable in his hatred toward me. "Get out. The grownups are talking."

"I'd watch myself, if I were you. I've got Jamie's body now, and something tells me he could take you." I turned to Charles. "I need you to think of a whistle. Invent one if you have to. I need a whistle that can draw Pesta out of this guy. Maybe like something to draw out poison? Or a version of what you use to strip the curse offa Foss?"

Everyone stopped what they were doing and gave me their full attention. Alrik's eyebrows wrinkled. "What do you mean, dear?"

I pointed to the poor newcomer. "Parts of him are still here. His body's still working. Pesta's not all of him. Just a part. Is there a way to separate out the foreign matter?"

"We need information from him," Foss argued. "Even if that were possible, we'd need more than a halfy to do it. We have to know how Pesta's finding us."

"Oh, yeah? How's that working for you? Why don't you chop off this poor guy's arm and see if that makes him more vocal." I turned to the guy strapped to the chair with blood dripping down his forehead, cheek, shoulder, arms, fingers and thighs, and pooling around his feet. "You know there's a person in there, right? One of yours, Foss. He's not in control of his body! Do you think he can move his mouth to tell you anything? No! Pesta's pulling his strings."

"But how?" Jens asked, turning back to the man covered in sweat and blood.

"I couldn't care less how it's happened. Point is, it's done. You can't keep hurting him like this! He won't be able to tell us anything until Pesta's out of him. That's what you should be focusing on." I moved closer and put my hand on the man's forehead, tsking him when he snapped his jaws at me. "Now, now. It's okay. What's your name?" I knew he would not tell me, but it seemed wrong not to at least ask. Stringy long black hair and brown skin to match Foss's, but the yellow eyes were from Pesta. I bent down to look at him square on, pressing my hands to my knees so I could examine the fervor as he lunged for me to no avail.

He screeched so loudly, I knew it had to hurt his poor vocal cords. I placed my hand on his forehead, my heart breaking for him. "I'll call you Harold until you can tell us your name, okay? Now Harold, I don't want you to worry. The guys'll stop hurting your body. We'll get Pesta out of you." Then my eyes narrowed, a sinister smile I didn't often tap into creeping across my Jamie face. "And Pesta, if you can hear me, I'm a little insulted at what a poor job you're doing at catching me. I mean, I thought you wanted me, *needed* me. Your Weres just got schooled by a human. A small little girl." Then I blew a kiss just to taunt her. "I think I'll just kick back with the rake Hilda the Powerful ganked from you. Maybe I'll just throw it out, the piece of trash."

The poor possessed man snapped and foamed at me, his master clearly having got the message.

I turned to Mace, who looked up at me with black and silver eyes full of sorrow and regret. "I don't know what you think I can do, but I can't move a soul from a body! If I could, I would've fixed you and Jamie already. I would've helped Henry Mancini!"

"I know, big brother. But I have faith in you. You're a Kincaid. Or I'm a Mace. Whichever one. We're the same." I motioned between us. "When it hits the fan, we figure things out. I know you've got this."

Mace shrugged, looking more wiry now that I was thicker and taller. "Okay. Give me a minute. Let me think."

I placed my hand on his back to urge him on. "Pesta's the poison inside Harold. Try to suck it out with a whistle."

He shook his head, his hands frustrating his messy hair. "It's not that simple. I have to put the poison into something else. Even if I could do what you're saying, where would I put her poison? I don't think anyone would volunteer for that."

Uncle Rick breezed by me and opened the door. "Fetch me an animal, darling." He shook his head. "Um, Jamie. Sorry, grab whatever you can catch and bring it here, alive." His eyes twinkled as he turned back to look at me. "We may just be able to kill two birds with one stone, here." His hand rested on Mace, gripping with assurance that he believed in his boy. "This, you can do. I'm certain of it."

Jens looked uncertainly to Alrik. "Do you really think it'll work? I've never heard of anything like this."

"I'm always eager to find a new bit of magic that's yet to be discovered. Pesta's already bested me once today because she pursued new methods of planning her attack. I will not be limited by what I already know."

Foss shook his head at the waste of time, but kept his protest to a mere grumbling as he stepped back. "Have at it, Mace."

Jamie called to us, reeking of frustration. "I need some help, here. This body isn't cooperating."

Foss rolled his eyes at me. "You have never been more useless to me than you are now. There's two of you, and neither of you are doing me any good." He pushed open the door to help Jamie capture a wild animal.

Charles gulped, and I could tell he did not have much confidence in himself as he readied for the challenge. "Do you want me to do this?" he asked, dreading my answer.

"I think it's our only way. Don't think about Pesta in all of it. Just focus on the poison inside of Harold. He's sick, Charles. Can't you see it?" I placed my hand on Harold's head that was slick with sweat, ignoring how hard he tried to lash out at me. My touch was maternal, and I hoped that Harold could feel it through all the layers of crap between us. Poor guy. He couldn't have been more than thirty, and was bleeding because my boyfriend and husband couldn't think outside the sociopath box. I glanced up at Jens, who was staring at me with admiration. "What?" I asked.

"I just love you. That's all. Even through the Jamie, I can still see you."

I smiled at him, blushing at the compliment.

Jens barked out a laugh. "I've never seen Jamie look like that before. Are you actually blushing? That's like, totally cute that I do that to you."

I leaned back against the chair, my hand still on Harold's head to comfort him. "Whatever. I always knew you were gay-bones for Jamie."

"I can't wait to get you out of that skin, baby."

I grimaced. "Why do your compliments have to sound like Hannibal Lector?"

"Because I'm gay-bones for you." He grinned at me, despite the gravity of the situation and the fact that his reply made not a lick of sense.

Foss and Jamie came back in with a small pig the size of a wiener dog. Foss had tied its feet, and it squealed unhappily at me, as if it knew I was the person responsible. *I'm sorry,* I mouthed.

Alrik ordered Foss and Britta outside, lest the cramped quarters become too crowded with all the large bodies. They watched from the window, not willing to miss a moment of the birth of this new magic.

Mace waited until Alrik, Jens, Jamie and I had our ears sufficiently covered before he summoned up a four-noted whistle. We all watched with bated breath as Charles gave in to the side of him no one could suppress.

18

SACRIFICIAL PIG

*A*t first, nothing of note happened. Mace was zeroed in on Harold, who had not stopped thrashing next to me. I stood as his bodyguard of sorts with my hands over my ears, waiting for a glitch in the Matrix.

Then Harold stilled. Goose bumps broke out on my skin when Charles fell to his knees, belting out the whistle that was our only hope.

It was a thing of fortune that Harold was tied to the chair. His whole body went rigid, and then his chest puffed out, jerking him forward with violent force. The high-pitched screeching was replaced by a man's hoarse cry for help that we could not give him.

I looked over at Charles and saw that his nose was beginning to bleed. "Wait!" I cried out, hands still over my ears. "Charles, stop!"

He shook his head at me, belting out a fifth note that tied through the others like a braided rope, until it was all one string. The pain on his face was only matched by his concentration, and I immediately regretted this idea.

Before I could say anything more to stop him, a white spot gathered on Harold's chest. It was a light – stringy and ethereal, like alien spaghetti. It twisted like worms into a ball on his sternum, the strands fighting with Mace to hide from being taken from their stolen home.

Without breaking his tune, my brother pulled the white light from Harold's chest. It looked warm, like stringy taffy as he carefully moved it with shaking hands to the pig. Charles was pale and sweaty, his long fingers trembling to stuff every bit of the angel hair pasta into the thrashing pig's skin. His whistle changed to include only two notes before he collapsed on the floor.

I ran to my brother, picking him up and holding him in my beefy arms. "What have I done? I didn't know it would be that hard! I'm sorry, Charles! Wake up! Wake up!"

Alrik snatched me up off the floor, and Mace rolled away from me, unconscious. Alrik handed me a dagger and pushed me toward my body. "Jamie! Lucy! Kill the pig together!" he instructed, eyes wide. "He's got a soul now, but you have to do it together!"

The poor pig was having the worst day of his life, and then to complicate things, he squealed up at me with yellow eyes as his tiny mouth began to foam. "He's a Were!" I yelled, stating the obvious.

Alrik pushed me forward. "It must be done together, and it must be now. Go!"

Jamie understood the situation faster than I did. He yanked the dagger from me and wrapped my giant fist around his dainty one. We knelt together, and I'm not ashamed to admit that I closed my eyes and screamed as we plunged the dagger into the pig.

Something bigger than lightning shot out from both Jamie and I. It hit us with such force, we were blasted out and upward, hitting the wall as if we'd been shot from a cannon. The last thing I remember before it all faded to black was blinking away blood and seeing my uncle run to me with an expression of utter horror.

19

DEAD WEIGHT

*J*awoke to the most unexpected of sights. Foss had me in his arms and was... washing my hair?

I needed better hallucinations.

I blinked, but my world did not change. I was on my back, lying in the water as Foss cupped his hand and trickled the cool pooled rain over my forehead in the dim twilight. I lifted my hand to bat his away, but my limbs were not behaving as they should have. My body felt weighted and stretched, which was made all the more disorienting by the floating I was doing in the lake I had not taken myself to. "Foss?" I whispered. My throat felt like I'd screamed at a blaring concert all night and was paying for it now.

He shushed me not unkindly and continued washing my face. "We're not sure what that was, so don't bother asking." He briefly made eye contact. "Are you... you again? Did it work?"

Reality came slamming back into me in violent waves. I picked up my hand and fumbled around for my face, feeling my smooth cheeks and chin. Tears welled before I could stop them, and I reached for Foss, my arm moving far slower than normal.

"It's you. Okay." Foss did an uncharacteristically nice thing and wiped my tears away for me. "You're ugly when you cry," he informed me, his usual charm resurfacing.

"You're ugly," I retorted, but my speech was slow. My brain was chugging uphill, trying to force movement against brakes that were not going to ease up anytime soon. "Where are we?" I asked, taking in as much as I could in my periphery. My neck was stiff. It felt like I needed to ask every muscle permission before I used it.

"We're taking a break. Not a long one, but I can't carry Jamie anymore tonight."

"Wuss," I joked. It was then I realized Foss was whispering. "Why are we being quiet? Is something wrong?"

"The new guy isn't talking yet, but we had to get out of that house. The owners came back and weren't happy. Mace took care of them, so they won't come after us, but it was dicey for a while there. Jens got into blows with the man of the house."

I wanted to shake my head, but I only succeeded in dragging my chin to one side and leaving it there. "Can't really move," I informed him. I didn't like him hovering over me, but I couldn't exactly leave on my own.

"As soon as you're mobile, we're going. The others are still on the path. But if I can get you walking, Jens can carry Jamie for a while. Give me a break." Foss helped me to sit up, but I flopped around like a rubbery doll. He leaned me to his chest, and I located enough facial muscles to produce an adequate grimace. "Come on, Lucy. Try a little."

"I am!" I tried wriggling my toes inside my filthy, damp Chucks, but they barely moved. "What happened to me?"

"To both of you. When you and Jamie killed that pig, something happened. Not lightning exactly, but a huge flash of light that shot you both backward. It would've been entertaining if Jens and Alrik hadn't been so scared."

"Is Mace okay?"

"He's fine. What a baby. Uses a little of his magic and passes right out." Foss cupped a handful of water and dripped it over my face, rubbing out who knows what from my cheekbone. "We stopped so he could rest a minute. Sit here and I'll see what's what."

That's what he said, and then he dropped me in the water. I'm sure a normal person would have just sat up, but my muscles were so sluggish that I remained submerged seconds past my comfort level. Then I realized I couldn't get up and started panicking.

Foss pulled me out of the water, barking at me as if I'd

nearly drowned on purpose. "What are you doing? Stop playing around."

My head lolled back, and try as I might to operate my limbs, they were completely uncooperative. "I can't move right!" I fretted. "Jens! Get Jens."

"He went to go track down some *angelica archangelica* to bring you two back. You've been out for a while."

My eyes moistened again at being left at Foss's mercy.

He was gentler than I was expecting, maybe because he sensed a breakdown was eminent, and did not want to witness the atrocity that was my ugly crying. *Ass.*

"Calm down. Does anything hurt?" He had one arm behind my back, and the other under my thighs.

"No. I'm fine, I just can't move right."

"I was really hoping you could start pulling your weight. We've been walking all night, and it doesn't look like we're going to make it to the next village by morning. I don't want us out in the open if we can help it."

I leaned into him as he lifted me, a child in his capable arms. "Be careful. Something's off."

"You've always been a little off."

I had a retort all nice and ready for him, but I was so relieved to be back in my body again, all I did was sniffle into his chest as he took me back to the path with the others. They were sitting or lying against a gathering of trees in various stages of exhaustion. "Jens?" I called in a whisper.

Jens was on his feet and had me scooped from Foss's

grip in no time. I breathed much easier in the safety of his embrace. "You're back?" he asked, waiting with bated breath for confirmation that I was not still his best friend.

Foss rolled his eyes at us. "Would you calm down? You're making a scene."

Britta stepped over Mace's feet and ran her fingers through my hair. "Lucy? Jamie? Which one?"

"She's back, in all her annoying glory." Foss took Jens's post beside Harold, who sat off to the side looking like a giant frightened bunny.

She picked up my hand and kissed it. "It worked!" she cried, tears falling into the well of my palm. "Are you well?"

I tried to wiggle my toes again, but still could not do more than a tiny jerk of the big one. I sucked down a steadying breath to stave off the freak-out I did not want to have with so many witnesses around. "I don't know. I can't really work my body yet."

"Just her mouth," Foss interjected. "Lucky us."

"Shut up, Foss." I could tell my speech sounded like I was drunk.

"Pop quiz," Jens said, not ready to kiss me again until he knew for certain it was me. "When is National Cheese Day?"

I leaned against his naked chest, hoping he would never wear a shirt again. He was such a thing of beauty. "Every day should be National Cheese Day. C'mon, Jens. Everybody knows that."

Anxiety he had not clued me in on rippled out of him

as his chest heaved. He sat down on the muddy grass, my body clutched in his protective vice grip, and used my neck as if it was an oxygen mask. "I'm so glad it worked!"

"I thought you were fine with making out with Jamie for the rest of your life." I found my arm, but it was weighted and clumsy when it tried to comfort him. It flopped on his back and bounced like rubber twice before it dragged across his shoulder. I guess it's the thought that counts, because Jens held me with yet more covetous affection. "It's alright. I'm here."

Jens permitted Alrik to kiss my wet hair, but no one else was allowed near. In the elation from him, I felt the fear he'd held back. In that fear, I began to understand how dear our fragile fledgling of a relationship was to him.

Foss broke the happy moment with tensed shoulders and a whisper everyone knew to respect. "Something's on our trail. I can feel it." He sniffed the air at the same time Jens did, and the two communicated something the rest of us were unaware of. "We're moving." Foss hefted the still sleeping Jamie across his shoulders with a determined expression to muscle past the discomfort. "Faster, if we can."

Jens stood with me in his arms and nodded to the path. "You set the pace, then. You're the one with the load to carry."

Mace sidled next to me, a hopeful expression on his pale face. "I can take her, if you need a break."

"No, thanks," Jens answered, not even pausing to feign

consideration of the request. "You're barely upright as it is. She's fine. We can have a little reunion when we reach Elvage."

Mace did not argue, but I could tell he was unhappy.

We walked along in the dark for a long time. I was amazed at Jens's strength to carry me for so long, but I was blown away by Foss. Dude was an ox. Sweat poured off him, but he led the way without complaining until I could see his legs trembling.

"We have to stop," I commanded. "I can walk now, but Foss is ready to pass out!"

"I'm fine!" Foss called over his shoulder in a quiet voice that carried just above our footsteps. "Alrik, where did you say your friend lives? Are we even close?"

"Not too far now, but Lucy's right."

"I can take him," Jens volunteered, setting me down gently so I could test my legs before putting too much weight on them.

Foss needed no more persuading. He set Jamie in the mud and stretched before he fell down on all fours beside the prince, and then collapsed onto his stomach with a groan.

I made some squeak of concern and stumbled toward him. "Foss!" I knelt in the muck that was so deep, it was up to my thighs. I rolled him over and picked his head up out of the squishy brown. "Wake up, buddy." I slapped his cheek as Mace helped me to sit him up.

Charles did not need to be asked, which was good,

because I wasn't going to require more of my poor brother than I already had. I covered my ears as Mace pursed his lips and sent a quiet whistle to Foss. I waited until he was almost finished before sneaking a hit of the energy he instilled into Foss. Just that little bit I let seep into my ears was enough. I could feel it in my toes, up my spine and all throughout my being. It felt as though even the molecules in the air surrounding me crackled and popped with electricity and potential. I dropped Foss's head without thinking and was sucked into the lure of the whistle. There was no danger, no one else in my universe, and nothing that could not be overcome as I stuck my ear to Mace's mouth, my eyes rolling back at the sound that wooed me.

When Jens ripped me away from Mace, I couldn't even focus on their argument; I was too dazed. My muscles were useful again and alive with just enough youth to get me moving on my own. I scrambled to my feet and pulled Foss up to sitting. The whistle worked on him to a degree and even made Jamie stir a little, but I was more susceptible.

Alrik pointed to a cluster of homes not too far off. "There. I'm sure someone can give us respite." He and Mace helped Foss to his feet. The father and son carried Jamie to give Foss a break, and Foss was given the cord that had the bound Harold at the other end of it. Harold watched me as I walked between my boyfriend and my husband. Try as I might to feel secure next to Jens, I knew I would not feel safe until I made sense of the new addition.

20

DARLING HUSBAND

"Not that I agree with it, but I can totally see why the Huldra were banished. That was a little scary, big brother. Getting the owners of the house to lend us the place, and then making them think it was their own idea? Brilliant." The effect of Mace's whistle on me was starting to mellow out after the trudge up the long hill to the village at the top. I wanted to sit my weary body down on the nearest chair in the long house. There were probably more comfortable ones somewhere, but I couldn't commit to the effort of locating them. It was only the fact that I was caked in mud from my butt down that stopped me.

Charles grinned, proud of his prowess that was growing the more he used his whistle. "I'm getting better at controlling the strength of it," he declared with a puffed out chest. Foss and Jens regarded him with wary expressions, though no one complained that they were out of the rain. "Some people just enjoy walking in the rain to their relatives' home. The lady of the house said it was only a mile away. That's not terrible."

I sent an air high-five to Charles, but I think that only confused him. "Just don't try anything like that on us. The force is strong in you. Maybe too strong."

Charles raised his hand in promise. "I vow to only use my powers of persuasion for the good of the mission."

Various groans and moans accompanied the clamor of boots to the wooden floor. The family had already stoked the fire, and Alrik made quick work of adding more wood.

Britta held my hand and led me to the bathroom, not waiting for the men to offer us the chance to wash up first. My clothing peeled off with a slurpy sound that was akin to something farting out of a condiment bottle. "Gross! I would throw my clothes out, but I've only got a few changes here. When we get to the Other Side, you and I are hitting a mall."

"Jens is getting us clothes from the house. He'll leave them money. Normally I would object, but I can't take much more of the filth, either." Britta ducked under the bucket, and I trickled water over her head. We spent a thorough amount of time washing ourselves, knowing full well that the men were impatiently waiting.

Jens had set a pile of clothes for us just outside the door. I was so grateful for the clean garments, I didn't even care that they were dresses. Well, Britta wore a proper nightgown that belonged to the lady of the house. The only thing Jens could find that wouldn't fall right off me was the preteen daughter's dressing gown. It was beige and fell to the middle of my shins. My boobs were obviously bigger than the eleven year old's, but other than that, I didn't stretch it out too much. I felt kinda childish, playing dress-up in a child's slip, but I was past being embarrassed. One day, I'd be a woman again with boundaries and a real bed, not one of the guys who slept on the floor and didn't own a brush. Luckily, the lady of the house had two house-coats that sort of looked like thin dressy bathrobes. Britta donned the red one, looking like royalty, and I threw on the emerald green one. It was a foot too long, but I didn't care. Britta helped me roll up the sleeves. It kinda felt like wearing a dress-shaped king-sized bed sheet.

Britta and I relinquished the bathroom and brushed each other's hair by the fireplace, the serenity only inter-rupted by the occasional splash outside and pathetic moan. "Is Foss outside?" I asked Mace, who was still in line for the bathroom.

Charles nodded. "He's using the second wind I gave him to try to get information out of Harold."

"What?" The moan became more clearly heard as a groan for help. I leapt to my feet and scampered outside, immediately peppered with more rain. "Foss! You get inside right now! Leave him alone!"

"Go back in, Lucy. He's our only shot at getting inside Pesta's head." He dunked Harold's head underwater in one of the rain barrels with his giant muscles that punished with renewed strength.

"Stop!" I screamed, running with bare feet to him through the mud. My heart pounded, and the icy rain pelted me like fat fingers falling from the sky that was one thick gloomy cloud.

"Get inside!" Foss ordered again. "And put some real clothes on!"

I tried to wrestle Harold away from Foss, but if you can imagine, I lost. I did manage to dodge Foss's backhand, though. "Please, Foss! Don't do this! Just give me some time to talk to him. If that doesn't work, you can try again." I grasped around for anything to win the argument. "Don't you want to dry off? Go inside. I'll make sure you get the bed tonight! I'll... I'll make dinner for you! Just please let me try."

Foss hesitated as he held Harold up by his arm. Harold looked so pathetic; I couldn't allow Foss to work him over any longer. "He won't tell you just because you ask nicely. This isn't a tea party, Lucy."

I took a risk and placed a hand on Foss's muddy back. "If that's true, you can have him back when I'm done. Please. If I was your real wife, wouldn't you do whatever you could to make me happy?"

Foss spat on the ground. "You're not my real wife. You're the bane of my world."

Back at you. "I don't ask for anything. I'm your only chance to be married. Please. I saved your life twice. Do me this one thing." I tapped my chest where his ring rested, an eternal reminder that I was a dead man's property. "This hurts me. You're breaking my heart hurting Harold like this. You should protect me from things like this."

Foss stared into my eyes with a hard expression I never expected to change. "Lucy, I..."

I rubbed his back, feeling the ache in the firm muscles that were slick with sweat, rain and mud. "You're so tired. You've been through so much. Let me help you. Remember how I helped you with the boat? The nets? Let me help you now. Go inside. Get yourself clean. Rest up a little. Let me handle Harold for you. You work so hard." I laid it on thick, but in reality, every word was true. Foss did work hard. He'd carried a full-grown huge man I don't know how many miles through mucky terrain. I leaned up on my toes, pulled him down and kissed his cheek. I could feel his exhaustion and the adrenaline that was ebbing. "Let me take care of you now. You can take care of everyone else in the morning."

Foss's shoulders drooped, a dramatic sweep that dropped Harold to the ground with a splat. The bloodied newbie was smart and stayed there, the sole witness to Foss brushing his lips to mine in a kiss that could only be described as grateful, and yet was somehow still platonic. He nodded, pressing his forehead to mine. "I'm so tired," he admitted.

"Then let's get you cleaned up so you can go to bed." I

gave up on the notion that my robe could be salvaged and hugged Foss, bracing myself when he sagged against me, nearly knocking me over. "Whoa! Okay, buddy. Inside with you." Foss nodded, and allowed me to lead him into the house like a puppy. "Jens, could you go get Harold cleaned up? No more hurting him. I mean it. I'll talk to him and see what I can find out, but he's been through enough. Get him some clothes and help him wash up in the rain bucket outside."

Jens nodded, standing from the designated mud spot near the front door. He was next in line for the bathroom, but sacrificed his spot for Foss, who looked half-dead and wholly beaten down.

Jamie had bathed in one of the rain barrels outside just so he could hurriedly clean himself and turn in. I tapped into my psychic link and saw that he and Britta were taking advantage of their rare moment of privacy in the master bedroom. I checked out of the link right quick before I eavesdropped on their alone time.

Charles exited the bathroom freshly bathed and wearing clean trousers borrowed from the man of the house that were a little too big on him. "All yours." His tired grin met mine, and I could tell all of us would sleep well tonight. It had been a long time since we'd had a home to rest in. The crackling fire was a luxurious treat that proved a great comfort to the group.

I ushered Foss into the bathroom, expecting him to release my hand so he could have some privacy. Instead, the giant beast of a man pulled me into the small space with a lost expression that told me he wasn't together enough to put thoughts in a proper order.

I took pity on him. He was too pathetic to take care of himself, but too proud to ask aloud for my assistance. "Do you need help?"

Foss just stared at me, and in the dim candlelight, I could see bags under his eyes and a haunted look I wasn't sure would ever go away. "What?"

"Okay. Sit tight, darling husband." I offered a small smile he did not return as I got down on my knees and ran a rag around the large steel basin, washing out as much of the leftover mud from the previous bathers as I could in one pass. I turned on the spigot that was connected to one of the rain barrels outside and ran a few inches of water in the tub. The emerald robe I wore was thoroughly wet and muddied, so I unhitched the belt and let it fall to the ground, hoping I'd be able to get the stains out. The child's dressing gown I wore was only barely damp in spots, and totally devoid of dirt.

When I turned around, I noticed that Foss still had not moved. I stood in front of him, but he didn't see me. It was a sad thing to watch someone so big and powerful be reduced to a shell of a man who couldn't string words together.

Slowly, and with fingers gentle enough to stroke a child's face, I coerced Foss to stand in the center of the bathroom. I had already seen him naked before, but this time I wasn't angry at him for it, nor was I embarrassed as his trousers fell to the floor. I helped him into the tub and lowered him down. As I poured the cup of water over his head and started to wash his hair, Foss began to cry.

Silent tears I never expected to witness drooled down his cheeks, collecting in the water that was no longer clear. He made to cover his face, but I pulled his hands away. Finally the dam broke, and Foss clung to me, burying his face in my bosom and sobbing for all that he'd been through and everything he'd lost. The wall of bravery crumbled in my small hands, and I tried to be gentle with the damage he permitted me to carry for this brief moment. Behind closed doors, Foss trusted me. When there were no witnesses, he allowed himself to be a person.

He pulled away after a good ten-minute breakdown. We said nothing of it as I washed him, caring for him as if he was my husband. The tender time we spent in the bathroom was special to me. I treasured the small moment I was allowed to be there for him. This would most likely be my only chance to have a husband, and I was determined to do it right.

I picked up the hard soap and drew circles into his shoulders, noticing the tension there. My small hands worked on his large muscles, hoping to rub a bit of power back into them. He moaned at the pampering. Jamie was a big guy; it was no wonder Foss was in pain after carrying him for so long.

When he was clean and his shoulders properly

massaged, I reached for the razor on the sink. "I don't really know how," I admitted. "Teach me?"

A mild dose of life lit in Foss's black eyes. "You don't have to. I don't know why you're being nice to me."

I kissed his forehead, leaving a mark of love on him he did not move his hand to erase. "I want to. You should let me be good to you. It's what friends do. If I was your real wife, we'd be friends. This is what I'd do after you'd had a hard day."

"Okay." He still looked lost, but he found me in his darkness, which was a start. "Thanks, then." He nodded and pointed to the powder and bowl on the sink. He shook a bit of the white powder into the bowl and mixed in a small amount of water until it made a fluffy paste. I spread it over his face, rubbing his jaw to relax him further, taking time to be gentle. I wondered if anyone had ever shown him how to be kind.

In the dim light, I learned how to shave my husband. His soundless tears streaked the shaving cream, but neither of us addressed them. It was a delicate dance we did, but we were learning to be good to each other.

I rinsed his face, wiping away the last of the cream to discover a freshly shaved, but still defeated man before me. "Tell me it gets better," he whispered, "having your life burned away."

I nodded, running my fingers through his short hair to soothe him. "It gets less painful after a while."

"I don't know how you do it. I lost everything."

I tapped his bare chest. "You're still you. They can't burn that away. I'm still me. No matter how many of my homes Jens had burned to the ground, I still take me with me everywhere I go." I gave a perfunctory chuckle. "Though, I didn't have nearly as much to lose as you did. Every move, I lost more and more. Now all I own is stuffed into a backpack. Queen Lucy, indeed."

"How are you okay?"

I offered up a sad smile. "I'm like, the cockroach of survivors. I should've given up a long time ago. Not totally sure why I'm hanging on." I put the bowl back in the sink, gravity taking control of my shoulders and pulling them downward. I touched my Linus heart on my chest, hoping some comfort still remained in it for me. "I'm not okay, Foss. Most days, I'm barely hanging on."

"I know I'm already dead, but I feel like I'm slowly dying," he admitted. "Is that normal? Will it go away?"

I nodded, scooping up some water to rinse a few rogue hairs on his cheek off. "It dulls. Little by little, you find purpose in other things. This mission helps. When it's over, you'll carve out a new life for yourself somewhere. Start over. You built up a name for yourself once. You can do it again." I tapped my finger under his chin, raising it to instill a bit of self-esteem in him again. "You're a survivor. I have faith you'll make it. We're both too stubborn to let go completely."

The anguish in his eyes was hard to take, but I did not look away from his rare moment of weakness. He swallowed, and I noticed a stray bit of cream on his Adam's apple I missed. I wiped it away and swished my finger in the water. He touched my hand as he studied my face. "Why are you being nice to me?"

"Me being nice isn't actually a new thing," I informed him, standing to get a towel. "It's you letting me that's the shocker. You're growing. That's a good thing, darling husband." I stretched the towel out and turned my head as he stood, dried off and then wrapped the cloth around his waist.

He was giant in front of me. In the close proximity, I don't know why, but I was suddenly too timid to look up at him. I was damp and chilly, and he was nearly naked. "I'll go get you some clothes."

I turned to leave, but Foss grabbed onto my arm. He stared at me with sudden lucidity, as if a modicum of purpose was coming back to him. "I'll not forget your kindness this time. This… you… I don't deserve this."

I shrugged, casting up a simple smile at him. "Then make it your business to start deserving it."

Foss stilled, his eyes looking past all the things that irritated him, and he finally saw me. He drew me closer, and though he had been much more naked seconds ago, I was very aware of his lack of clothing as he examined the curves of my face. With one hand gripping my arm and the other cupping my cheek, Foss raised my chin and kissed my lips lightly, just once, and let me go. "It wasn't a mistake, making you my wife."

Lucy! Jamie yelled in my brain. *You'll not carry on like this!*

I pushed Jamie out my mental door and locked it tight. The same confusing explosions rippled through me, coloring my cheeks and making me take a step back to right my messed-up brain. I put my hand on the knob and steadied myself. "Easy, tiger. Get some sleep. By the time you wake up, I'll have Harold all sorted out for you."

Foss wiped his hand over his face. "No. I'll help you."

"He won't talk to you. You're the great Master Foss. He's terrified of you, but he's got that Fossegrimen stubborn streak. You can't beat information out of someone like him."

"Maybe *you* can't," he jabbed. "Take Jens, then. And put on some decent clothes that aren't completely transparent."

"Well, it wasn't see-through until you got me all wet," I defended myself. I softened under his wistful gaze. "Look at you, caring about me. Goodnight, darling husband."

Foss cracked a sliver of a smile. "Goodnight, lovely wife."

21

HAROLD

Jens and I sat across from Harold, who was tied to a chair at the kitchen table, not saying a word. Harold had a black eye, split lip, and was covered in bruises from Foss, who was passed clean out on the bearskin rug in front of the fireplace. Mace was asleep in the young girl's bedroom, and Jamie and Britta had long since retired to the master bedroom.

Jens was exhausted, but he stayed by my side as I sat with Harold, who was not speaking. Alrik tried starting up a conversation several times to no avail, and I could tell he and Jens were growing frustrated.

I stood and rummaged through the cupboard, pulling down a cup and filling it with water. I placed it in front of Harold and sat back down. "Guys, give us a minute. You're both tired, and I'd like to talk to Harold alone."

"Lucy, I don't think..." Jens argued.

"Just go lay down by the fire. Uncle Rick, make Charles share his bed. It's not like Harold's going to hurt me. You're all right here if I need you."

It was obvious Jens wanted to protest further, but Uncle Rick offered his hand to Jens, enforcing my offer. They were all so sleepy. It didn't take much to convince them to let me handle things. The living room where Foss slept and where Jens would retire was right next to the kitchen, and in perfect shouting distance. I wasn't scared. Maybe it was foolhardy, or maybe I was just that tired. Either way, it was clear Harold wasn't in the mood to talk.

Once we were alone in the kitchen, I lowered my voice. "If I untie you, will you behave?"

The man who had remained unresponsive throughout the entire trip and interrogation focused on my face and nodded slowly.

"So you do understand us. Good." I stood and moved to his chair, crouched at his side and worked on undoing the knots that were much too tight for proper circulation. "Did Foss tie you? That's awful. That's gotta be uncomfortable."

Harold nodded again, and I could feel him studying my every move as I fiddled with the knots.

"Sorry. I suck at this. Give me a second." My fingers pulled, and slowly the bindings began to give. "I've been calling you Harold, but it's only because I don't know your actual name. Do you feel like telling me who you are?"

Harold shook his head once.

"That's alright. Harold's fine by me, if you don't mind it."

Harold shrugged.

"I'm Lucy. Well, when you first met me, I was in Prince Jamie's body. Long story, but I'm me now. Not that you know who that is." I sighed. This must've been the frustration Foss felt when I stopped talking. "You understand me, but you won't talk back?"

He stretched his neck and shook his head again.

"You can't talk?"

Harold nodded vigorously.

My heart tugged. "Oh, man! You poor thing! Foss was trying to get answers out of you, but you can't speak. I'm so sorry." I succeeded in releasing his left arm, and watched with trepidation as he moved his large wrist around. It was a dangerous game I was playing, setting loose the man who tried to kill us, but it seemed the right way to go.

Harold reached for the cup, his hand shaking. I met him halfway and molded his fingers around the vessel. Then I helped him tip the cup to his lips. He trembled as he swallowed, and I wondered just how injured he was.

"Is anything broken? Can I help you?"

Harold gave a noncommittal shrug, which I took to mean, "Sure, kid. Help me out a little."

I wetted a rag and put it to his lip, dabbing at a spot of blood that had not yet dried. He was big, like the others, but the poor guy looked so defeated, I wondered how crappy his life had been before Pesta got her hooks into him. "Can I ask you about how Pesta possessed you? We're all kinda curious."

Harold shook his head. It wasn't defiance; it was helplessness. The poor guy truly had no answers. His ponytail had come loose, and long, greasy strands of hair swayed at his cheeks.

"Can I ask you about your life before she stuffed someone else's soul in you? I mean, that's pretty crazy. You're just walking along, and bam! Table for two? Were you aware of what your body was doing?"

Harold nodded, morose. He hung his head to show his noncompliance with Pesta's commands.

"Dude, that's rough. So she had someone else in you that she could control? One of the souls in Be?"

Harold nodded again, moderately grateful that someone was catching on.

"Have you always been mute?"

He shook his head.

"So, this is a new thing since Pesta took over, huh." I observed his utter defeat and tipped the cup to his lips again, brushing his hair back from his face. "That's good news. Maybe your voice'll come back after your body adjusts. Then you can tell us your name."

Harold did not look like he had much hope in this. He mouthed, *can't remember.*

"Can't remember what? Pesta? The other soul?" I could see his frustration as he tried to push me to understand. Then it dawned on me. "You can't remember who you are?" He nodded vigorously, and my heart sank. "You don't recall anything before Pesta, do you?"

I hit it on the head, and finally we were on the same page.

"Do you know if you died before she put a lost soul into you? Or did you cross over to Be and she snatched you up there?"

Be, he mouthed.

"You're young," I observed. "Maybe late twenties? Early thirties? I thought Be was a place mostly for retirees. Your life must've been pretty grim if you turned your soul over to her so young."

Harold shrugged with a hollow look in his eyes that had nothing to do with the beating Foss doled out.

I knelt beside him, having given up on untying the crazy knot on his other arm. I looked up into his obsidian eyes and tried to communicate with utmost sincerity that he could let his guard down with me. "Pesta screwed you over pretty good. You didn't want to attack us, did you?"

He shook his head in earnest. Then he began struggling against the binding on his arm and legs, letting out a small raspy whine.

It was a good sign. He was capable of noise. We were getting closer.

I tipped the cup to his cracked lips. "The things you must've seen. You didn't want that life. You went to Be because she promised an escape. She lied to you." I wasn't trying to hide my hand. I wanted him to know the point I was gunning for so I didn't spook him. When it seemed we were on the same page, I held his free hand between mine and rubbed his wrist to soothe him. "Harold, I need your help. Pesta keeps finding us, but I don't know how. She sends Werebears, of course, but she's been possessing other animals. And now you? It's too far. It has to end." I massaged his forearm, and I could feel him relax in my grip. "Is there any way you could help us?"

Harold found himself through the haze of relief I was instilling in his arm and nodded.

Crap. Yes or no questions were the only thing he could handle right now. I thought hard on how to best pull the information from him.

"So, she's tracking us, right?" His nod prodded me forward. He pulled his arm from me and pointed to my forehead. "In her mind? Some psychic way?"

Harold shook his head, frustrated with his shortcomings. He pointed to my chest.

"Me? She's tracking me? What the crap for?"

Harold pounded his fist on the table once, and then mimed stabbing himself in the heart.

That was pretty clear. "Oh. To kill me. That sounds about right. Why wouldn't she hate me? Never met me, but whatever. How, though? How is she tracking me?"

He pressed his finger to my forehead again.

"In her mind?"

He shook his head. The bags under his eyes and his various injuries were evident, even in the candlelight. I may not have beaten him up, but I realized questioning him when he was in such a sorry state was cruel.

I rubbed his arm again. "I'm sorry. You're just as tired as we are. How about I give you some time to get your voice back?"

Harold nodded gratefully, his shoulders sagging forward. His mouth hung open, too swollen to resume its proper place.

"Hang in there. I'll get Jens to bust you outta these. My brother's a Huldra, so he might have to whistle you to sleep so we can be sure you don't escape, but no one will hurt you."

Harold shook his head and began to cry silent tears of desperation.

I stood and ran my fingers through his black greasy hair, pulling his head to rest on my hip. "It's alright. I'll stay with Foss. I promise no one will attack you here. Foss shouldn't have done this to you. I'll make sure it doesn't happen again."

Harold tossed me a look with such resignation to his fateful death, I couldn't not hug him. I was considerate of his many sore spots, but did not otherwise hold back. Poor kid. Sure, he was far older than me, but he looked like a giant boy all beaten down like he was. I kissed his forehead, somehow making him cry even harder. "It's okay. It's alright. Let it out." I patted his back gently and held him for several minutes until he was able to collect himself. "You have to trust me a little bit, here. Let me get my brother. He won't make you do anything you don't want to do. He's just going to help you sleep through the night." I brushed a lock of his long hair from his face and tucked it behind his ear. "I'll be here when you wake up. Promise."

I pressed one last kiss to his temple before rousing Mace and summoning Jens. Jens was reluctant to untie him, but he knew Harold had no weapons on him. Jens was sleeping in the main room with me, so there was precious little opportunity for Harold to escape.

Charles was tired, but luckily whistling an exhausted person to sleep was fairly simple. Jens and I dragged the poor guy into Mace and Alrik's room, depositing him gently on the wooden floor. Jens tsked me when I retrieved a spare blanket from a closet and covered Harold with it.

"You're such a mother," he commented, bumping his hip to mine with a sleepy smile.

I snorted and then yawned. "Well, our little giant's going to be okay. Please don't let Foss in to see him in the morning. I'll probably wake up if he does, but just in case."

Jens kissed my lips with great tenderness, his pace slow and drippy, like the candles that did their slow melt around us. When he finally pulled away, fifty percent of my problems magically decreased. "I love you," he whispered. "When this is all over, we'll sleep in a real bed together." He glanced into the main room toward the fireplace where Foss rested on the fluffy rug. "Without Foss."

"Agreed." I pulled out two more blankets and moved toward the hearth. I got down on my knees and stretched the smaller of the sheets over Foss, making sure to cover his toes and tuck the cloth around him without disturbing his slumber. I laid down next to him and patted the spot of fur on my other side. "Come on."

Jens was always beautiful, but clean and shirtless, he was a sight to behold, even as tired as I was. "Baby?" he whispered as he slid in next to me and pulled me to him, facing me and taking full advantage of the fact that very little material separated us. He kissed my lips once before he spoke. "I saw you kiss Foss outside."

I stiffened, my eyes flying open. Suddenly, I was fully awake and ready to go for a run – a very long run away from this conversation. "I... um... yep. I did. It didn't mean what you're thinking, though. It wasn't a romantic kiss."

Jens shushed me, which normally I'd take issue with, but this time I let him take the lead. "I know. I saw it. Looked more like kissing your dad than what we do." He kissed my scrunched nose. "You told me we weren't together, and I get it. I just didn't want you to think you had to hide anything from me." His long arm stretched down and cupped my calf. Then he took his sweet time dragging his hand up the back of my thigh, his thumb dancing on the edge of danger. "I only want to be with you, though, so I guess I'll just have to be patient." Goose bumps ripped up and down the length of my legs, and I shivered. Jens smiled lazily, fully aware that I was his plaything, and he was a very naughty boy. "Do you want to be with Foss?"

I was acutely aware that the subject of our little

hushed conversation was right next to me. I could feel the heat from Foss's body warming my back. It felt dangerous and wrong in so many ways. "Of course not. We've just... we've been through a lot. Neither of us feels that way. We're trying to figure out how to be civil to each other." I closed my eyes, the guilt I'd suppressed tearing at my insides. "It didn't feel wrong because it felt like friendship. Like, our version of it. Is that completely mental?"

"Not mental. Not normal, either. But that's Foss. You're good for him. And surprise of surprises, he's letting you be good to him. If it was anyone but you, I'd be happy for the guy."

"We're just friends, and sometimes barely that. I know it sounds weird, but I'm his wife. I kinda feel responsible for him."

"I know. You've got that mothering thing in you." He kissed my lips, hitched his leg around mine and rolled me atop him so he could tease both my thighs. "Do you want Foss?"

"Of course not," I breathed between his lips. The firelight lit his tanned skin in luscious ways, the glow bouncing off his perfectly toned body. "I only want you."

He kissed a line down my throat, and my entire body felt like a powder keg teetering on the edge of an explosion. My back arched involuntarily, and before I knew it we were rolling around in front of the fireplace, a mess of arms and bare legs. We panted and gasped as the stakes were raised, the heat of the fire lighting our bodies in all the right and wrong places.

When Jens kissed me, I felt alive, like life was possible and worth making a grab at. I mashed my lips to his, letting loose a tiny squeal when he was not so gentle with me. My legs locked around his as we rolled off the rug, tangled and seeking each other at new angles while still trying to keep things quiet.

I noticed Foss stirring out of the corner of my eye, and the air in my sails began to dissipate. "Shh," I scolded Jens as he lifted my skirt to an indecent height. I rolled off of him, giving him space to deflate as he stared up at the ceiling, trying to catch his breath.

Foss rolled onto his side, muttering with his eyes closed. "Go make babies somewhere else. I'm tired." He scratched his cheek. "And Jens, you're acting like a child. Of course Lucy's still yours."

I covered my mouth to stifle my giddiness. "Sorry. Go back to sleep." I adjusted my gown so it was more appropriate and laid down in between the men, smiling as Jens situated himself.

After a few more goodnight kisses, I fell asleep sandwiched between the two warm bodies. One day, I would look back on this journey and the oddity of this sensation would dawn on me. That night, however, I could feel nothing but safe, and that blessing was a rare commodity.

22

———

JUST AN ACCIDENT

"I lower my guard for one second, and you let this happen?" Foss roared in the cramped space of the bedroom. "Where's Alrik? He'll answer for this, that's a sure thing."

"Mace and Uncle Rick are hunting for food. They'll be back," I informed him, trying to keep a cool tone to calm the situation.

Poor Harold sat on the bedside, his head hanging as he readied to receive the beating I promised him would not come again under my watch.

Jens waved Foss's anger off like the man was an annoying pet. "Give it a rest. Nothing happened. Harold's still here. No one was attacked. We covered all our bases."

I'd explained Harold's muteness and that everyone needed to back off, but Foss was in a state. Letting his guard so thoroughly down last night had serious repercussions. Every time I spoke, I could feel his anger boiling. I had cared for him. I had bathed him. He'd kissed me. He'd thanked me and been kind. It was a situation he would make me pay for, I was certain.

"You! I expect this from her, but you?" Foss growled at Jens, his nostrils flaring.

Jens rolled his eyes. "Unclench, Foss. You're just pissed because we did something without talking to you first. She breathed without your permission, too. Yikes."

Foss lunged at Jens, and I screamed. "You two are obnoxious! Knock it off!" It was tight quarters for the alpha dogs to wrestle in. As soon as they reached the doorway, I pushed Foss out the door and slammed it shut behind them. I ran to Harold and knelt in front of him. "Is your voice back yet?"

He was able to eke out a whisper. "Yes."

I held his hands and begged him with probably too much passion. "Please tell me something I can take back to Foss. He's not going to calm down unless I can prove to him it was a good idea to spare you." Harold nodded, and I squeezed his fingers. "Good! Now tell me how Pesta's tracking us. Tell me why. Tell me everything, quick!"

"She's hunting you so she can finish the portal on the Other Side. It's almost done. She's just missing a little more bone. The structure isn't useable yet. She needs your bones." He paused to cough. "She's keeping tabs on Alrik because he's an elf, and they leave traces of magic that can be tracked. She thinks some of his magic is in you, so she's following scents of that around, sending Weres when she gets a whiff of his magic in the air."

"B-But I'm not magic! I'm one hundred percent human. Alrik's not even my real uncle! We're not actually connected." Then I inhaled sharply when I recalled that, thanks to Alrik's *arv*, I now was his blood relation.

"It's you, Alrik and the Huldra boy she tracking, though she doesn't really care about the boy's bones. She wants your bones, and she's going past her territory to get them. She's got the other animals she's not supposed to be able to control, too." His face was morose as he spoke, begging for clemency. "When I crossed over into Be, she told me I could keep my arm and still stay with her in paradise if she could use my body for just a little while. She kissed me, and I felt something cold – part of her – slide down inside me through my mouth." He shook his head. "I didn't know! I didn't think she'd make me do all the things I did!"

Foss came charging back into the room, and I sprang to life. "No!" I threw my body onto Harold, wishing with everything in me that it would deter an attack. Foss ripped me off Harold and launched me hard against the wall, knocking my head to the wood.

I always thought "seeing stars" was just an expression, but I had to blink away the small bursts of light that accompanied Foss's temper. He bent over me, always surprised and confused at my smaller stature, and was shouting something with grave concern in my face.

I heard Jamie cry out, and Jens ran into the small room and leaped atop Foss, punching and kicking until the two were a tangle of masculine nonsense on the floor. I stood on unsteady legs as the room shifted. Harold caught me and pulled me across the bed, steering me to the doorway so I didn't get hurt anymore. The room shifted unnaturally, like I was instantly drunk.

"I'm sorry!" I clung to Harold, who nursed the left side of his body as he led me out of the bedroom and into the kitchen. "I thought I could protect you from him. I promised I'd keep you safe. I'll figure out how to settle him down. I'm so sorry, Harold. Are you alright?"

Harold nodded, fingering my face and showing me a trickle of blood that stemmed from my hairline. I'm not sure if it was the head wound, the sight of blood or just plain bad luck, but gravity pulled at my body like a vacuum trying to suck me into the center of the earth. Harold caught me and lowered me to the chair at the kitchen table just as Jamie stumbled out of his room with Britta.

"Did-ja do this to her?" Jamie roared, his speech beginning to slur.

Harold shook his head, but Jamie wasn't looking for an answer. He took a swing at Harold, but his aim was so impaired, the momentum knocked him off-balance. Britta placed her hand on Jamie's back, and I could feel the irritation flaring up in him at being babied.

"Jamie, stop!" I cried. I was so dizzy. I swooned off the

chair, heading straight for the floor. Harold caught me and righted me at great personal sacrifice to his own injuries. We were a sorry state, the whole lot of us. Britta was the only one with her wits about her, but she had no idea who was in the wrong or how to be helpful.

Vomit churned in my gut, and try as I might to steady myself, I knew it was no use. "Outside," I begged Harold, who was surprisingly the only one apprised of the situation. I began heaving and only just made it out the door as the bile retched out of me. Jamie crawled to my side and puked up his dinner.

I was cold as the morning rain pelted down on me, my white dressing gown soaking through in half a minute. Harold looked down on us, putting together that we were laplanded, and now there were two pathetic messes to look after. "Run, Harold," I coughed out as my stomach slowed its purging. "I can't keep you safe. Who am I kidding?" I wiped my mouth. "I can't even keep myself safe! Run."

He looked on me with pity and pushed out in a rasp, "Where would I go?"

"Anywhere. It's a fresh start. Pesta can't control you, now that the foreign soul's out of your body. Go now! Foss is... just go!"

Harold debated this, looking around for what I assume would be an escape route, but his eyes landed on me and he shook his head. "No. I can't leave you like this."

I sat up and sagged against the house, watching in fear

as Jamie collapsed in the mud. "It's too late for me. I'm in it, and I'll never get out. Run, Harold! Please!"

Harold smoothed the hair from my face and kissed my forehead. "Thank you, Guldy. Move quick to keep ahead of Pesta. She knows you're headed for Elvage. The Mouthpiece is waiting for you there."

Then Harold stood, gave me an unfathomable look and turned from me. He limped off down the hill, aiming toward the neighboring village. As I watched him go, a small amount of my anxiety decreased. It was too late for me, but Harold had a chance at a new life. He would escape and start over.

When a large hand I would know anywhere grabbed my shoulder, I screamed and burst into tears. Given the circumstances, I don't think that was an overreaction.

"Get in out of the rain," Foss scolded me as if I was being annoying on purpose.

"Don't touch me!" I shouted.

"Calm down. It was an accident. Let me see."

"Jens!" I yelled, my own volume making my head swim. "Jens!"

Foss helped Jamie up and lifted me out of the mud, carrying me into the house. I struggled against him, and Britta shockingly came to my aid. She punched Foss square across the face. His head snapped to the side, and when it rounded on her, it was with the disposition of a bull seconds before the charge.

Jens emerged from the bathroom, sporting a fresh

shiner. "What the... I know you don't need to be told again! Leave her alone!"

Foss glared at the siblings. "It was an accident, I already said! I'm trying to make it right, so back off!"

"Put her down!"

The two mules yelled their frustrations at each other until the noise and chaos started giving me a migraine. I fought against Foss until he set me down. Then I pushed my way past Jens to the bathroom in my tipsy state. I was so tired. My skin felt thin and my bones, breakable. I turned on the spigot for the rainwater and filled the tub halfway. It seemed I could not escape the mud. I peeled off the ruined gown and stepped with leaden feet into the steel basin, slipping twice, but luckily catching myself before I fell.

Frustration welled up in me and tipped me over the breaking point. I sobbed into my hands as I shivered in the cold water. I was a stereotype. The woman with the abusive husband she swore she could change, but who ended up putting her in the hospital anyway. It was always an accident. She was always the one who tested his temper, and somehow when he damaged her, she blamed herself.

I would not be the Lifetime Movie of the Week. I would not hold out any more hope that Foss could be saved. Uncle Rick may not give a crap about my life, but I wouldn't go out like this. I wouldn't be thrown across the room, and I certainly would not...

My head felt fuzzy, like a halfway broken television set

you have to bang on the side to get an image to appear. The room started to tilt again. I was so tired. From the day, sure, but also just from life. I washed my face and my arms, but nothing seemed to rouse me.

The world was grim, and just as I suspected, love did not conquer all. Try as I might, I could not make Foss a better man. My love was just as useless as Uncle Rick's.

My eyelids drooped, and I laid down in the foot of water to get comfortable. I could feel an alarm going off in what was left of my brain, but my body was too weighed down to care.

23

___

HEAD INJURY

*T*he weight of the world pressed down on my chest. Over and over it shoved itself into my sternum until... water? Something wet gushed out of my lungs and onto the floor.

The burning sensation I unfortunately was already familiar with scorched my esophagus as I struggled to pull in a breath. As the world came into focus, tears leaked down my cheeks. I had not died. I was still in the stolen house, and stood no chance of checking out of the mission early.

Jens sat me up, face ashen, and held me to his chest. "She's breathing!" he announced, his voice cracking.

Foss sat up from hovering over Jamie's body and pulled him upright. His relief was plain as he steadied Jamie. Britta was in a right state as she hugged her fiancé.

"You hit your head," Jens explained unnecessarily, "and

then you both went to sleep and we couldn't wake you up. I didn't put it together soon enough. Concussion. Then you went under the water." His chest contracted with relief and the extreme elation that only comes after you're released from a paralyzing fear. "Whew! You're okay. You're okay." It felt like he was reassuring himself more than me, the sweet guy.

I became more aware of the situation when the towel Jens had wrapped around me slipped a few inches, snapping each man's head in my direction. Jens and I both fumbled to cover me, but I was already too wrecked to deal with further embarrassment. I sagged against him and shook my head, the pain still fresh. "I can't do this," I admitted. "I can't be here anymore. Take me home. Please, Jens. Take me home."

Jens evaluated my besotted expression and nodded. "I'll see what I can do. You're right. This isn't safe." Securing the towel around me, he stood, lifting me off the ground. He addressed the rest of the room's occupants. "I was hired to watch over her, not to tear down the portals at any cost. She's done more than enough. I won't lose my charge for the mission. We're out." He ignored the floored expressions and carried me to the nearest bedroom, kicking the door shut behind us.

24

THE NEW PLAN

"I can't believe I let it go this far. I'm sorry," Jens muttered as he laid me down on the child's-sized bed. He kissed my lips, begging for forgiveness and a second chance as he sat on the side of the bed, one arm on either side of me. "I'm the best Tom there is, I swear. Your family hired me for a reason. I don't know how all that got so turned around. All of it, my fault. We'll figure this out and take you home."

"I'm sorry." I sat up on the bed so I could whimper into his firm shoulder. I could feel the muscle beneath and knew if that bulk couldn't keep me from concussion in Undraland, nothing would. "I'm so sorry. I want to help. I want to be a team player. It's just too much. I can't live like this anymore!" I planted a kiss on his neck as I cried quietly. "And now I'm taking you away from your home. You must hate me."

The towel covered my front, but it had fallen open in the back. Jens let his hand travel up and down my naked spine as his warm breath heated my neck. "Anytime you want to deliver bad news, always do it dressed in only a towel. For some reason, I'm not disappointed at all." He mustered up a smirk as I cinched the towel tighter around me with a faux scolding look. He rubbed his thumb over my cheekbone. "But seriously, I shouldn't have put you in this position. Your parents didn't tell you about Undraland because they wanted to keep you away from all this. I thought... I was wrong. End of story."

I touched my aching head. "I need to take a nap. I'm so tired. Then can we leave?"

Jens shook his head. "No nap for you. You've got a concussion. Get ready for a long night of ghost stories and my loud singing to keep you awake. You love country music, right?"

I groaned. "What about Jamie? How can I leave? We're tied. He's not going to go along with this." Depression weighed down on me. So close to freedom, yet always so far.

Jens hugged me, kissed the cap of my shoulder and traced my spine under the towel. "Let me handle Jamie. In fact, let me handle everything from now on. I should've been doing this in the first place." He squinched his eyes shut in shame. "I can't even count how many times I left you alone. Left you with Foss! You make it so easy to forget my job. It's that moxie you've got. Being with you..." He kissed my throat, sending shivers through my very aware body. "I'll take care of it."

He kissed my forehead and released me, warning me with a look not to lay down or do anything that remotely resembled sleeping. "Britt, come keep Lucy company. I need to talk with Jamie."

Britta stood with her brother in the doorway, whispering back and forth with serious expressions. Jens left us, and Britta set to work doing what she did best – being awesome. She fished out a pair of my clean clothes from Jens's red bag and helped me dress when I got too wobbly. We did not speak until I was fully clothed and we were both sitting on the bed.

"I'm sorry," I whispered, hugging my knees. Jeans felt so good on me. My purple tank top fit me like the glove I needed to breathe properly. I looked more like myself, and therefore, felt more like myself. Funny little system.

Britta shook her head. "We'll go with you. Jamie doesn't have anything to stay here for, except maybe me. And I'll go if that's what's best. I haven't felt at home in Tonttu for a long time." She fiddled with a thread on the sheet. "I'm worried I'll have trouble in your world. You made fitting in over here look so easy. I fear I'm not as flexible as you."

I scoffed. "Well, that's overly gracious. And a lie. Everywhere I've gone in Undra, I've stuck out from a mile away."

Britta managed a weak smile. "I imagine that's how you were in your world, as well."

I returned her smile, the sweetheart. "I'll help you. Don't worry about that. Uncle Rick will find a way to undo the lapland eventually, and then you and Jamie can go wherever you want." My face fell. "That is, if Uncle Rick'll still talk to me after I jump ship on him."

"He'll survive. As much as we all believe in the mission, it was his to start with. He's asked too much of you. I said so to my brother from the start."

Jens returned, nodding to his sister. "It's done. Jamie's agreed to go over to the Other Side as soon as Alrik and Mace get back, and you two feel up to the journey. It's still a ways through Bedra. Then we'll have to pass through a portion of Elvage to get to the doorway in Tomten. At least a week's journey. Can you handle waiting that long?"

"Of course. Thanks." I breathed for the first real time in ages. "Thank you." I squeezed Britta's hand. "Thank you. You're an amazing friend, Britt."

She kissed my cheek and excused herself to go keep Jamie company.

"Thank you," I breathed to Jens once we were alone. "Thank you."

"You said that already. You're welcome for finally doing my job." He waved off my forthcoming words of gratitude. "Enough serious talk. We've got years for that, and you've already scheduled us for couple's counseling, right?"

"Yes. In five years, I plan on giving you a thorough tongue lashing."

Only Jens would have the gumption to find dirty

humor in that. "Tongue lashing, eh? That sounds..." He raised an eyebrow at me and sat on the bed to kiss me. "So we've finally got a bed, but we can't sleep on it." He played with the spaghetti strap of my tank top and kissed my shoulder, smirking at my shiver. "What could we possibly do to pass the time?"

If you can believe it, we managed to fill every minute with enough of our own version of tongue lashing to properly redefine the term.

25

THOMAS JEFFERSON

Foss had not spoken in two days. It was just as well; no one wanted to talk to him. They all knew his temper was the ultimate reason I was leaving and taking more than half the remaining group with me.

We trudged through the mud, but since the rain had stopped, it all felt less dismal. That, plus I was going home. I respected my uncle's somber mood and kept to myself for the most part. I did not relish the parting of ways. It was just time. As much as Uncle Rick said he understood that, he treated me different. There was less indulgence in his eye, and he had not called me sweetheart since we left the cabin. Now I was Lucy.

I could accept that. He was Alrik to me now, anyways. He'd stopped being my uncle sometime after the golden boars when he didn't march me straight home. I didn't fault him for it, but it was our usual passing friendship. He would come into my life for a weekend and then leave. I'd lasted who knows how long in his world. Mission or not, I couldn't stay for him anymore.

Charles forsook all pretense of building a cool friendship with me. He held my hand all hours of the day until a meal or sleep forced us apart. I'd given him the option of coming with me, but didn't fault him if he wanted to stay. I understood, but I wouldn't purposefully abandon him. He still had yet to make a decision.

We ate in silence that evening, as we had the one before. The small fire crackled in the night air, lending a small bit of luminescence to accompany the blood moon I wasn't sure I would ever get used to. "I'll miss that," I admitted quietly to Charles as we chewed our crumbly biscuits. "That red moon's a hundred times the size of ours."

Charles squeezed my hand. "Then stay. You don't have to go to the Other Side. You can come back to Elvage with us. Live with me. Stay, Lucy."

It was not the first time he'd begged. It was not the fiftieth. I shook my head. "If you understood the wonder that was chocolate ice cream, you would know why I can't do that." I tried shtick, but it fell flat. Jens rubbed my back, and I leaned into him.

Alrik turned in without saying goodnight or even looking at me. Jens noticed the slight and shook his head. "He'll get over it. Once he comes up with a contingency plan, he'll forgive you."

"Forgive me?" I tried not to take offense, but it was impossible. That he might not forgive me for going home was irrelevant. I was still working on forgiving him for putting me in such danger in the first place. "Let's go to bed."

Jens kissed me and set on clearing the rocks away from the heat source so we could have a decent place to lay on the damp ground. He hadn't done that before. Jamie did it for Britta from the beginning, but Jens let me clear my own space. Then it dawned on me that I wasn't one of the guys anymore. I was a woman.

It was nice.

I told you he'd catch on, Jamie voiced in my head.

Foss went for more kindling as Jens spooned me and the others wound down for the night. I grinned as Jens whispered all the normal things we would do when we got to the Other Side. "Chinese food. Gobs of it. And escalators. Can you imagine Jamie freaking out on one of those?" He sniggered into the nape of my neck. "We can get a killer car and go for drives to nowhere."

"Blast the radio?" I suggested.

"Not your music," he amended. "But yeah, music, food and my girl. Not much else we'll need."

"A bed," I whispered, speaking the true desire I had gone my whole life wanting, but never getting. "I want a bed in a house that we don't have to move from. I want a white picket fence and a friggin' garden with tomatoes."

"I can help you with that." He wrapped his leg around

mine, caging me with his body so I was completely embraced. I felt loved, and for the first time, like someone was listening when I spoke. I ached to go home and start a life with Jens.

He kissed the back of my shoulder. "I'll get you your picket fence. I'll build you a good life. Promise."

We both stiffened when we heard Foss's footsteps running toward us instead of walking. Paradise began to crumble as the immediacy of our current world descended upon us. Jens was on his feet by the time a harried Foss reached the fire that had died down to embers.

"Circhos!" Foss announced, catching his breath. "Everyone up and get ready!"

Alrik gathered up his things and pulled out a sword, making my heart thud unevenly in my chest. "Head inland to the water! It might still be deep near the center of the plains!"

I knew better than to ask questions. I could read Foss well enough to know that Circhos equaled big scary bad guys. Anything that frightened Foss was enough to get me on my feet and running alongside Jens.

"We're too late!" Britta exclaimed, pointing past the thicket to our left. She drew her dagger from her apron. "Jens! Your knife! Jamie, grab your bow!"

Jens turned, ripped open his pack and tossed his sister a second dagger (yes, tossed. OSHA would've thrown a fit). He stood with a sword in one hand and a curved knife in the other. I wanted to ready myself, but I had no idea what was coming, and no one thought to give me a weapon. I stood behind Jens and tried to make myself invisible.

I looked up and saw a sight so strange and horrifying, it scared the scream straight outta me. A... something came staggering out of the woods with a bloody bowling ball in his hand.

I didn't think there was anything short of a troll that could be taller than Foss, but there he stood. Fresh from the Michael Jackson *Thriller* video was a ten-foot tall WWE wrestler. His skin was charcoal black, but in the moonlight I could make out intricate red etchings all over his naked body. They weren't tattoos. The red marks were under the black layer, like the charcoal skin was a bark on the tree that was his deformed crimson body.

Jamie shot him with an arrow, but it only made his janky walk more off-center without slowing him down at all. The Circhos ripped the arrow out of his bicep like pulling off a stray hair. His left arm and foot were small, almost my size, while the other side was appropriately proportioned for his body. He walked like a zombie, but when he growled, he showed off fangs that were too long for even a vampire.

He stalked forward, ignoring the arrows ricocheting off his armor-like scales without causing more than a nuisance to him.

In my large assortment of monster movie viewings I'd participated in over the years, my dad always teased me for my emotional state afterwards. I got a chill, sure. But I was more upset about the monster. He was usually the only one of his kind, and everyone wanted to murder him. People screamed when they saw his face, and he never got a word in edgewise. Who knows? Maybe the monster was an excellent chess player or had a flair for restoring old automobiles. We would never know, though, because all we saw were the layers of makeup that convinced us he was no good, and that fear was a viable option when confronted with something different. Maybe that's why I had patience with Foss, and why it hurt so much when I gambled on the monster and lost.

The poor mess of a giant zombie came at us with determined precision. He sucked on the bowling ball and whined out a growl that made the hairs on my arm stand up.

Then it hit me. Britta was nearest me, so I grabbed her sleeve and tugged her to the gathering of trees to our left. "I need a squirrel or something."

"A what?" Britta asked, her face pale.

"An animal. Something! Get me something he can eat. That's all he wants. Give him some meat, and he'll be happy."

Britta shook her head, trying to aim her focus in one direction. "I, but there's nothing around here. Critters know to scatter when a Circhos is around. Plus, there was just a flood! I can't just summon one, Lucy!"

"Brilliant! We'll summon one." I kissed her cheek and ran back to the mayhem. Alrik was spraying the Circhos with hot water that shot out of his palms, while Jens and Foss were wrestling it. "Mace!"

Charles closed the distance between us, and I could see the terror in his silver-black orbs. "Go! Run with Britta along the path. We'll catch up."

"Can't you whistle him down?" I asked, jerking my head to the bloody scrap of men and beast.

"Circhos don't have ears." His head whipped back to the fray. "Run, Lucy!"

I held his hand to focus him. "I need a pig or a bunny or something. Can you summon one of those?"

"What? Lucy, go!"

I shook my head. "First get me an animal. Something easy to kill. Can you do that?"

His frustration with me was so rare; it was hard to recognize at first. He wiped sweat from his brow and tried to focus. "Fine, but then you run."

"Like the dickens," I agreed. Britta moved between us and the beast, though we were a safe distance away for now. Mace whistled two simple notes, and I could tell in the succinct tune that he was scared.

I heard Foss cry out, and my heart raced anew. Uncle Rick was shouting, and Jens was grunting as Jamie tried to be helpful without getting both of us hurt in the process. It was madness.

Seven kanins came mindlessly scampering toward us, hopping in a direction they did not understand with their bunny ears, raccoon bodies and squirrel tails. They looked at each other like, "What the crap are you doing here? Don't you see the dangerous human female? Girlfriend's gonna make coats out of us."

"It's like living with the friggin' pied piper with you around," I commented, marveling at Mace's talent. "Okay, Britta? Can you kill them? Is that too scary?"

Britta shook her head and stabbed downward. I closed my eyes on instinct as the seasoned farmer and well, sister of Jens butchered all seven kanins that had no choice but to let her.

The scent of blood worked quicker than I could've hoped. The Circhos untangled himself from Jens and Foss, as if he had been tolerating their antics, but now daddy was tired of wrestling and wanted some dinner.

My hands felt small and incapable as the black tree bark zombie twice my size ambled toward me. His teeth were gnashing, but his focus was not on me. His eyes followed the trickle of blood that dripped down the gray fur of my little bunny in my outstretched hand. "Here, sweetheart. Are you hungry?" I offered the meat to him as if it was the last of my milkshake, and I just didn't care for it anymore.

Inside, I was screaming and sobbing and blubbering to Linus all the things I wished I would've done in life.

The Polyphonic Spree. I'd never seen them in concert, and now I most likely never would.

I'd never tried calamari because it looked disgusting,

but now I wished for the chance. Who knows? Maybe it tastes like Skittles.

I'd never finished *The Hunchback of Notre Dame*. That wasn't so much a regret of mine, but now I'd never know if the end of the book was worthy of being upset I'd missed it.

I kissed my unimaginative dream life goodbye and welcomed the nightmares that would come as Circhos progressed in his drunken stalk toward me. He made a noise that sounded pleased, almost like cooing and purring all at once.

As he reached me, I could see more details that made my welcoming smile feel that much more forced. He had three toes on each foot, and the smaller foot was definitely around my size. We could've shared a blue Chuck Taylor, for sure. His fingers were gnarled, but as he moved his arms, I realized that they moved in lightning-fast scissor kind of motions. He was bald, and one eye fit his head, but in keeping with his manky foot and arm, his left eye was smaller. "Well, you're just a cutie." I beamed my bravest smile at him and set one of the bunnies down between us.

Bald Zombie Edward Scissorhands looked at me as if to size up my sincerity in offering him the gift. No doubt he was the one on the playground that the kids offered to play tag with, but really it was just an excuse to tape a "stupid" sign to his back and run away laughing, while no one did you a solid and told you it was there. *Been there, buddy.*

It was then I realized he was alone. There was no

Deformed Monster and Guest at our little party. I'd eaten alone at my fair share of lunch tables when Linus was out for chemo. I kinda hated it. It brought about a stigma in middle school that was hard to shake.

I could see Jens and Foss catching their breath and trying to make sense of what captured the attention of their newest wrestling buddy. As if in slow motion, I watched both of their faces twist in horror as they bolted toward me like sprinters with a bullet chasing them. "Lucy, run!" Jens yelled as he charged.

"No!" I commanded, holding my hands up to stop them. "He's just hungry."

I couldn't think of a proper name for him, so like always, I went with the first thing that popped into my head. "Go on, Thomas Jefferson. It's all yours."

I'm still not sure why I did it, but something compelled me to sit down, legs folded across from him to show him I was no threat. I also wanted to instill a bit of civility to the moment. As there was no table to eat at, we made do with the spongy wet grass.

Thomas Jefferson turned as Foss and Jens approached and swatted at them, sending both warriors flying backward to the shore that lapped nearby.

Britta was crying, and Jamie was yelling at me in my head and aloud, but I ignored them all. There was no one else in the world but me and Thomas Jefferson. I tried not to tremble as I pushed the kanin closer to him, reminding him of the gift.

I nearly sobbed aloud when Thomas Jefferson sat down across from me. It was an effort destitute of grace, but I beamed up at him that he humored my rules of proper table manners.

Thomas Jefferson reached for the bunny, watching me for any false moves as he brought it to his mouth. My smile remained fixed in place to cover over the terror that was racing through my veins.

Foss and Jens regained their footing, but they were too confused by what they saw to act. They obeyed my wishes and gave us a little space.

Watching Thomas Jefferson eat was a true test to my delightful hostess demeanor. He did not pick away the fur, but gnawed his way through it, discarding the bones only after he sucked all the meat and blood away.

"What's the plan, Loos?" Jens yelled. I could tell he was still thinking of a way to overtake the Circhos by force.

"He's hungry. Look around you," I said in a cheery voice with my smile still stuck to my face. Lucky Thomas Jefferson had no ears and couldn't hear our conversation. He could only sense my disposition, so I kept it light and cheery. "The rain's limited his food source. He doesn't want a fight. He wants food." I nodded encouragingly as Thomas Jefferson looked to me for approval. "Poor baby's starving."

"You're going to get us killed!" Jamie argued, livid at the risk I was taking.

"I'm pretty sure we were losing the fight anyway. Did

you want me to stand back and let him kill Jens and Foss first? He was coming for the git with the arrows next." I offered Thomas Jefferson another bunny from my stash, dropping it between us. He gathered it with his smaller arm onto his lap with covetous affection for the meal he had not been able to find on his own.

"Lucy, he's going to eat you next!" Mace exclaimed.

I shrugged. "Then I die. It's not like all of you didn't know this was a possibility. I don't fight, and I'm useless with all this outdoorsman kind of stuff. Surprised I lasted this long."

"Just stand slowly and back away," Jens instructed.

I ignored him. "Everyone listen to me. Mine is the only plan that hasn't gotten anyone beaten up. Jamie, go as far as the link will let you. Everyone else, just go."

"Lucy, we won't leave you here," Uncle Rick protested in his best impersonation of someone I obeyed. "You're eating with the equivalent of a zombie or a Yeti!"

"Well, I don't believe in Yetis. I have a plan. May not be a great one, but either way, just go. If I die, I die."

"Then I die!" Jamie argued.

"Then you die. Same as when you ran out to fight the golden boars in the Warf without considering what it cost me. You did the right thing for the group, and now it's my turn," I answered succinctly, grinning at Thomas Jefferson as he broke a bone clean in two with his teeth. "You had to know death was a possibility. You weren't exactly besting him earlier. And Uncle Rick, putting my life in danger's exactly what you've been asking me to do this entire time. Don't act all concerned now." I took a steadying breath and kept my calm smile in place. "Now, go. I mean it. He doesn't trust you."

"As soon as the kanins are gone, he's coming for you," Charles warned.

"There's not much in me worth eating," I joked, though it was a forced humor that fell flat. "I donated part of my liver, buckets of blood and bone marrow to keep my brother alive, and he up and died anyway. Maybe it was my parts that killed him." For some reason, I choked out a nervous laugh I'd been holding onto ever since Linus died. "I can't really explain to you what it feels like to go through all that and still lose your best friend, but I guess it tends to make a person a little reckless. So, go. If Thomas Jefferson eats me, he'll probably die, too. Problem solved."

No one moved. I probably should've been pissed that they didn't obey, but I was touched they wouldn't let me die alone. Somewhere between earth and Undra, I'd made friends. A little family of misfits that somehow banded together when we needed a proper fit most.

Jens's tone was soft, like a cop trying to talk a jumper off a ledge. "Lucy, honey, you didn't kill Linus. Your bone marrow kept him alive way longer than he would've lasted without it."

As if he could sense my pain, Thomas Jefferson broke the bunny's neck and ripped its head from its body. I smiled kindly as I let out a muffled scream. Then he did the sweetest thing any monster had ever done for me. He extended his hand and offered me the head. I could tell he was starving, and that this cost him dearly.

I didn't have the heart to turn away his gift. "Huh. Not so much a monster after all. Thank you, Thomas Jefferson." I took his generosity in my hands and put it to my mouth, doing my best to convince him we were sharing a meal. Thomas Jefferson bared his fangs to me in what could only be described as a smile.

"What the... What is she doing?" Foss marveled.

"Stay away," I ordered in a pleasant tone. "He hates you all for hurting him. Plus, I don't feel like laplanding with any more of you. I'll handle him by myself."

Jens spoke into the hand that was covering his mouth. "Baby, only you could get a Circhos to come to a tea party. How did you... you're amazing."

I had nothing to say to this. He didn't know my end game, and I doubted he'd have that dreamy eye for me after that. "Please go, guys. You don't want to be here for this."

"Are you going to make him your new puppy?" Charles asked, forcing levity into a moment so tense, you could pluck it like a fiddle's string.

"No. My wolf's dead. I'm going home after this. He's your big, bad monster for this region? I'll handle it so your world can be safer, and then I'm going home." I slowly stood, jerking my head toward the ocean that was gently lapping.

Thomas Jefferson stood, limping after me with his half a rabbit he was nearly done with. He roared at me when I stepped into the water, but I smiled up at him as if I didn't have a care in the world. I dipped my rabbit in the ocean and washed it off, showing him the nice, clean meat that was easier to get at.

I moved a few feet into the body of water, rinsing off the others as he watched curiously from the shore. He was afraid of the water, and I understood why. With one side of his body too small to carry him, I guessed he could not swim. Poor puppy. I waved him forward, offering another bunny to bring him out to where the water lapped at my knees.

He took a step into the water, breathing unevenly. He roared and screeched again, but when he saw that I was safe where I stood, he moved forward, eyeing the lapping waves with great trepidation. I cooed to him, urging him toward me with words he could not hear.

When he snatched at the bunny I offered, I turned facing out toward the moon. Big, enormous and red, the craters absorbed what little light they could and gave depth to the overwhelming sight I was certain I would never forget. I pointed to the orb and pretended to eat my bunny head. My finger slicked over the eyeball, and I nearly vomited into the skull. The horror mixed with the moment of peace and made for a blur of understanding between us. The moon was beautiful, and we were having a picnic. Aside from, well, everything else, it was a lovely moment.

Thomas Jefferson's munching sounds involved a fair amount of slurping and grunting. He breathed like a chubby guy, though he was all muscle.

I took a risk, ignoring Jens's shouting and Charles's pleas to come back, and stepped forward. Thomas Jefferson watched me walk until the water was up to my neck. I kept the floating bunnies clearly visible.

Thomas Jefferson walked out to me. The water lapped at my chin, but only came up to his waist. Call me a prude, but I was glad his monster man area was covered up at last. Took my level of awkwardness down a notch. I handed him a bunny, and he rewarded me with an expression akin to a smile. It had too many long teeth, and instilled a fear in me I would never get over, but sure enough, he was pleased with himself for braving the wild and making a new friend.

Despite everything, I was proud of him, too. I understood why he didn't care for the water, and why the flood was a greater danger to him, even with his muscles and superior height.

I grinned at him, picking at my bunny skull's fur, deciding which parts would fit into the Zone diet as he slathered and drooled over his. He had blood dripping down his face and hands, which I tried not to be terrified by.

I pointed to the moon again, ignoring Jamie's shouting

in my head. I pushed out everyone's fear and instructions so I could communicate with my pet Yeti.

Thomas Jefferson looked at the moon while I talked, knowing he could hear none of it. It was our own private moment, and I was determined to give him a good last meal. "We don't have a moon like that where I come from."

He glanced at me, pausing from his feast. Then he decided to give up any pretense of listening, since we both knew he couldn't hear me anyway.

"I wish I could tell you how much more I trust you than Foss. That you probably need a friend even more than Charles, or that I can see you wouldn't put me near harm, like Uncle Rick does. I get that."

He discarded his carcass and pawed at mine, kifing it from me with his scissorhands. He pulled away the fur, cracked open the skull and handed it to me, pointing to the delicious brains inside I could tell he was salivating over.

Huh. He really did understand friendship better than most.

Not one to be a jerk when someone did something kind for me, I scooped out the brains with my fingers and bent my head down so he didn't catch me not eating my dinner. I got a fair amount of blood on my chin and in my mouth and nearly cried, but swallowed it down with the fear and grinned up at Thomas Jefferson.

He gave me another terrifying smile, his wonky small eye gleaming that he'd been able to help me out.

He trusted me, which made it all the worse.

The last step of my plan required a steadier hand than I had at the moment, but I muscled through anyhow. With my gaggle of bunnies clutched tight in my hand, I pointed to the moon and began swimming towards it.

He followed after me for a few paces, but when the water touched his chest, he stopped. Whining like a grizzly bear, he beckoned me to come back.

I needed him to follow me. There was no other way. Foss couldn't take him down. Jens got thrown around like a rag doll. Until I left Undraland, they were mine to protect, and there was no way Thomas Jefferson would just let them go after they proved such an annoyance.

Instead of turning back to him, I swam a few feet further out and took a risk I was unsure would pay off. In a theatric performance that could be seen from the shore, I let go of the bunnies. "Oh, no!" I cried, pointing my most sad and scared face at my new friend. "Help me! They're floating away!"

I knew they would only float a few more seconds before they sank, so I pretended I desperately needed his help to retrieve them. It involved a lot of miming, a little begging and the lack of a soul.

Thomas Jefferson growled at the loss of food and threw himself past me. The water touched his chin, and he panicked, thrashing his large arm about and consequently pushing the bunnies farther out of his reach. He lunged for them again, per my instruction.

Then it happened.

Thomas Jefferson lost his footing and barely broke the surface as he tried to figure out how to tread water. With one side of his body shorter and less dexterous than the other, he whirled through the water like a T-rex, loud but ineffectual.

I cried as I launched myself toward the shore, kicking his head further down, depriving him of the oxygen he so desperately needed.

He'd needed a friend. He'd needed food.

I'd given him both for a moment before I killed him. The glitter of Undraland had turned to dust.

I swam toward the horrified men and the sobbing Britta. After looking over my shoulder to confirm that the lack of splashing meant my Yeti puppy was dead, I stalked out of the water, not meeting any of their eyes.

Walking past them, I saw the bloody bowling ball Thomas Jefferson had been carrying when he first attacked us. Upon closer inspection I realized it was not a ball at all. It was a head.

Harold's head.

I'd sent Harold away to save him from Foss. I'd sent him straight into the arms of my monster. Yet another death rested on my withering conscience.

"It's done," I breathed, marching past the flabbergasted group with blood on my face, ice in my veins and nothing in my soul. "Take me home."

LINUS

Once Charles had washed my face and sucked the water from my clothing, the others began recapping their favorite parts of the slow takedown. Foss and Jens cared nothing for their injuries, instead participating in the lively recounting of the events surrounding Thomas Jefferson's undoing. They asked questions, but I did not answer.

I did not speak. They were afraid of me beneath the awe, and they were right to feel so. I'd made a friend just to kill him. I couldn't think of anything worse.

They ate, but I did not. The smell of the stale bread sent my stomach heaving. I barfed up rabbit blood and the little food in my stomach a ways off from the fire Alrik had made for us to sleep next to.

Britta held my hair back and rubbed my spine as I sobbed over my puke. Angel that she was rinsed my mouth out with water from her canteen and held me to her chest while I cried. Jamie felt my self-loathing through the bond and lent his comfort in the form of a strong hand on my back. "It had to be done," he assured me. Together they held me while my white picket fence drifted further and further away.

This one took longer to suppress than the other horrors, but after ten minutes, I was sane again, at least as sane as could be expected. I tucked away my crazy and reserved my ticket to the therapist's couch that would happen in five years, after I had enough distance from the gore.

They led me over to Jens, who spooned me while I cried myself to sleep. Usually my dreams were a nice escape for me, and recently Jamie, as well. The pictures that plagued me that night were amalgamations of my recent experiences coming back to haunt me. I screamed as I shot my poor Thomas Jefferson in the face with a gun that I'd somehow convinced him was a bouquet of flowers. I tried with all my might to put him back together, but his blood only flowed more freely over my hands and arms. The blood turned into a red ocean that sucked me down into its depths, where the Nøkkendalig were waiting for me. I yelled for Linus to save me, but he wasn't there. He was never there anymore.

I fought against the blood river, panic welling up in me to the point of heart palpitations. Before the evil mermen seared their marks on me again, I was yanked up by a strong set of hands I trusted. *I've got you!* Jamie assured me, dragging me to the shore. *It's alright, Lucy. Honey, it's just a bad dream. I'm here.*

No! I cried. *Save yourself! You don't want to see all this.*

Jamie held me, and suddenly, I wasn't bloody anymore. I was dry and clean in his arms that held me tight. *I won't leave you, Lucy,* he assured me.

Then in the bushes behind Jamie, something moved. One step, then another revealed the sight that made me calm and sob simultaneously. *Linus!* I yelled, scrambling in desperation to my feet as I ran to by brother. My arms went around him, and even though it was a dream, I was finally me again in that moment. It was him before the last round of chemo, when he still had a little meat to him and short dark blond hair on his head. He was solid and strong in my grip, and I couldn't get close enough. *Linus! Linus, I knew you'd be back for me!*

He smiled in that I-just-stole-your-dessert-what-are-you-going-to-do-about-it way with hazel eyes that matched mine and said, *Well, obviously. You didn't think I'd let you go to the magical land of Narnia without me, did you? This place is nuts.* He looked around at the red moon, but I saw nothing except for him. *Speaking of nuts. What's got you all twisted? Is Jens being a jackwagon again? Want me to kick him for you?*

You knew! I accused him, laughing hysterically. My brain felt like it was filled with helium, the lightness lifting me beyond what I thought possible. *You knew about Jens and didn't tell me?*

I also know the lead singer's name of the Polyphonic Spree, but I'm not telling.

You jag! I laughed, my grin brighter than it had been in ages. I squeezed him tighter. *I've missed you.*

He held me with a matching smile and nodded to Jamie. *Who's Ranger Bob over there?* Linus asked.

I turned halfway to find Jamie standing awkwardly a few feet from us. *Oh, that's Jamie. He's in my head,* I explained. Though it was a dream, I swelled that Linus knew me so well that I didn't have to say more than that. He just got me, plain and simple.

Linus mussed my hair. *Poor guy. I wouldn't wish that bucket of crazy on anyone. Hey, man.* He greeted Jamie.

Jamie stepped forward and shook my brother's hand. *Good to meet you, Linus.*

Of course it is. I'm the prettier twin, he bragged. *This one time, I–* Linus stopped short, a confused look on his face. He jerked forward in my arms, and then stumbled back clumsily in confusion. Each step he took away from me, I noticed slight decreases in his appearance. He grew thinner, paler, weaker, and then his hair started falling out as he touched it, shocked that the follicles deserted him so easily. *What? What's happening, Lucy?! Stop it! Make it stop!* He freaked out and fell to his knees, vomiting in that awful chemo way. *Lucy, you have to save me!* he called out through the stomach spasms.

I threw myself on the grass next to him and held my brother while he gagged on his dinner. Jamie knelt down on his other side, searching for a way to be useful. *I'm trying!* I assured Linus, wracking my brain for a solution. *Take more bone marrow!* I ordered. *You can have it all!*

Linus stopped ralphing abruptly and yanked on my shirt. *It didn't save me last time! It's your parts that made me sick! Get them out! Get away from me!* Then my brother pushed me backwards, breaking my heart in two and keeping the good half for himself.

Lucy, this isn't real, Jamie insisted, trying to get my attention. *Sweetheart, you have to wake up now. I can't watch this.*

There was no drawing my attention away from the sight that was Linus. Gaunt, bald and bony, he was still a wonder to behold. *Linus, just give me a little more time. I can fix you. I promise, I can! I'll let you win at Tekken! I'll give you the good pillow! I'll... I'll...* I cast around for anything I'd not yet offered. *You can have more blood! Take as much as you need! Take it all! Please! Just don't go away again!*

Linus's face twisted in confusion. *I feel funny. Loos, something's wrong.* He touched his stomach, and then rubbed his eyes. When he pulled his hands away, his eyes weren't the identical shade of hazel as mine were. Linus stared at me with yellow eyes.

I screamed, wanting to run away from him, but unable to leave my brother. "No!"

Linus's descent into rabidity was swift, and took me to the Loony Bin five years ahead of schedule. My other half lunged at me, jaws snapping like a vicious shark. He ripped my heart-shaped necklace off me, and I screamed.

I couldn't fight him off. I could never hurt Linus or run from him when he was surly. Instead I curled myself into a ball and sobbed as he tore at me, removing bits of my flesh so he could eat it by the fistful.

Linus was hungry. I wanted to give him whatever he needed, but the searing pain of having layer after layer of skin ripped away was more than I could handle. He gurgled and growled as he grabbed for more of my skin.

"I can't! I can't!" I howled.

He was yanked from me by Jamie, who put Linus in a calm chokehold. "Lucy, it's not real, sweetheart."

"Don't hurt him!" I sobbed. My chest felt tight, and underneath the fear I could feel the beginnings of a panic attack. "I need him! I can't do this! Linus, I can't do this!"

There was a weight on my chest, and like water being let out of a bath tub, I was sucked out of the nightmare and dumped back into Undraland. "Shh, honey, it's okay. Wake up, Loos. Wake up!"

"I can't do this!" I shouted as I came out of my dream, my face wet with tears. "Linus? Linus? No!" My breath came to me in shallow puffs, and my fingers felt fuzzy as they grabbed for my necklace, holding the heart as I trembled and convulsed. "My... and he... Linus!"

Jamie sat up and ambled over to where Jens was holding me near the fire. I'd woken everyone up, but only

Jamie knew the depths of my broken psyche. "It's okay, Lucy. It wasn't real."

"It's your curse!" Foss accused Jamie. "It's been transferred to her!"

"Then we'll handle it!" Jamie spat back as Charles brought a well of water in his palm to my lips, forcing me to drink.

"Linus was... and then he was... And he died!" I sobbed into Jens's chest, the panic still gripping me as I replayed Linus's attack in my mind. "I can't do this," I repeated. "I just can't!"

"I miss him, too," Jens whispered, emotion swelling in his face.

Jens and Jamie did their best, but there was no comfort for me. I stayed awake the rest of the night, terrified of going back to the place where my brother had been a monster, and once again, I'd failed to save him.

27

NO MORE ROMANTIC NOTIONS

*W*hen the sun rose over the horizon, I did not feel the warmth. As it passed overhead and dipped in the west, I did not bother with the beauty of nature or the conversations that chirped around me. Everyone had something to say about the upcoming bout Alrik was expected to have with the portal, but I remained silent.

"You're quiet today," Alrik observed, walking next to me as if we were out for an evening stroll in the park.

I shrugged in response, not really wanting a rundown of what he thought about Thomas Jefferson's demise at my hands, or the night terror everyone had heard the bulk of. The others walked ahead, either sensing my need for space or allowing their growing fear of the monster I was becoming to drive their quickened pace.

Alrik stroked his gray beard. "I don't know the state of

Elvage. They must know of the other portals falling, and I imagine they have taken measure to counter any attacks they fear coming. The only way I will be able to get close to it is to pretend I'm ready to enter Be. It's a whole process, and I want you to be part of it."

I kept my mouth shut, but raged inside. I could not have been clearer when I told them I was out.

"You'll dress in the clothing of my people and send me off as if I was going away for a very long trip. Sad, but with the promise of reuniting when you yourself cross over to Be." He cleared his throat, put off by my silence. "One of the Toms, I can only assume Jens, will be carrying the rake using their invisibility. Once the guard is down and the portal clear, I'll take it from him and tear down the bones of my ancestors as quick as I can." He pointed to a blue flower that was nice to look at, but continued talking business while I fumed. "I am old, my dear. If one of the guards should interrupt me, Charles is part elf and my relation, so he is fit to finish the job. Jens will vanish him unless it's necessary for him to take over in my stead. It is my wish that you distance yourself from me if I am captured. Scream, cry and curse my name. I do not wish you imprisoned and stuck here."

I shook my head, finally opening my mouth, angry not at him, but at myself that he thought me such a pushover. "I told you people, I'm out. I'm going home. I'm not staying to send you off or tear down the portal. You don't need me for that. You didn't need me for any of this."

His voice was quiet. "When you first came to Undraland, I placed my star on your forehead. Do you recall that?" He traced his thumb on my forehead, mimicking the action I'd seen him do on Charles to revive him. I felt heat between my eyebrows.

"I remember."

"It made you my heir with Charles. So while you have your mother in your veins and your father, now you also have me." He paused to sneak a glance at my expression that was closed off to him. "So if I fail and Charles fails, you can also destroy the portal in Elvage, since you're my daughter. The bones that make up the portal in Elvage are my ancestors, and now they're yours, too, thanks to the *arv*. You still belong to your parents, and can still destroy the human portal, but now you can destroy both the human and the Elvage one."

My teeth ground together as I chewed on several angry retorts. Of course it was strategy. Of course he wanted me to be part of his real family now that it served his grander purpose. In my imagination, I saw Linus rearing back and socking my uncle-adopted-father guy. I swallowed. "I didn't ask you to adopt me. My parents are my parents. They kept me away from Undraland, and you adopted me just to bring me in? I'm your daughter now so I can destroy your portal?" I felt betrayed, and didn't bother masking the feeling from him for diplomacy's sake. "My dad would never let you do this. He was my dad because he loved me, not because I could be a tool to destroy something. If you wanted me because you loved me, you would've adopted me the day after I lost my parents, before there was anything in it for you."

Alrik nodded, having expected this to be my reaction. "I suppose if I assure you my love for you stretched long before talk of the portals became an issue, you wouldn't want to hear that, would you?"

"You suppose right." I sighed, feeling heavy all over. "Look, thank you for adopting me. Really, it's nice you..." I stopped. "I can't do this. I'm still out. I won't destroy your portal for you. And shame on you for using familial obligation to get me to do that. Actual shame, Alrik."

Alrik was quiet for a few moments as we walked over the spongy grass that backed up to the sand on the shore. The rainforest-like atmosphere was gorgeous, filled with lush colors and that freshly showered fragrance nature gets after a good storm. Though intellectually I could make these connections, emotionally I was detached. Too much had happened that took away my joy. I had no desire to pick flirty fights with Jens. I had little desire for anything except going home. Killing Thomas Jefferson so heartlessly absconded with my moxie, and somehow, I lost a part of myself in the transaction of our freedom for his life. Plus, I hadn't slept well, and couldn't shake the images of Linus.

"You're upset with me," Alrik observed.

"X marks the spot," I agreed. "Would you trust you after all this? Good for you for getting the job done. Let's leave it at that and go our separate ways. Adopt Foss or Jens. Then they can destroy the Elvage portal. Easy-peasy."

"I can't leave it like this." He shook his head while we walked, but I paid his concern no mind. It was too little far too late.

"You should have cared this much about me before we went on the mission."

"I did, Goosy. I still do."

"Huh. I don't believe you. You love me once a month, just like clockwork. I don't blame you for it. This Pesta thing is a big deal, and it's a good thing you're doing, standing up to the evil. But let's be real. I'm not the girl you tell bedtime stories to and sneak candy for anymore." I kept my eyes on the path ahead. "It's fine. I'm twenty. I'm just kinda done pretending that we owe each other more than the occasional monthly chat. You helped me move into a new place after my family died. I killed your Yeti. We're square."

"It breaks my heart to hear you talk like that. I planned on being better for you after your parents died. I wanted to be there."

"It's fine. I get it. I was clinging on to this romantic notion that you... But I understand now, and I'm done."

Jens fell back to walk with us. "I can see the gold dust up ahead. We're almost to Elvage. Loos, we'll pass by the portal on our way back to the gate to the Other Side. We'll be invisible when we leave the forest, so you might want to say your goodbyes now."

"Done," I answered succinctly. "See you, Alrik," I said cheerlessly, leaning up on my toes to peck his bearded cheek. "Have a good one." I did not permit a drawn-out goodbye, nor any additional emotion. It was my choice to leave and I did not regret it.

Alrik called me to come back to him, but I already moved ahead and had my arms around Charles. I kissed Mace's cheek and tried to echo the love I saw in his eyes.

"Please don't go yet," my brother begged me. "Just wait for me. I... you're making me choose."

I bit my lip, not having thought of Mace's dilemma in all of it. "Oh. Um, I don't want that. Obviously. I'm not ditching you. I just don't belong here. Come see me when it's all over."

His frown was etched into the hopeful face I'd grown accustomed to lighting up when we were together. "You can't wait half an hour? Don't fight with us. I understand if you don't want to fight, but don't leave me. Just stay with Jamie nearby." His volume dropped. "You promised you wouldn't leave me. I'm not ready to go over yet. I have to help Alrik do this. Just wait for me."

My shoulders drooped. "Yeah, I'm sorry. I didn't mean to go back on my word. Of course I can wait. Just don't ask me to help this time around. It's Alrik's thing. I'm out."

Mace's face began to lighten with renewed hope that I was not our parents, and I would not abandon him in Undraland. He hugged me, and I felt awful I had not considered him in the equation. I had been selfish, like

Alrik, and thought only of my mission. "I'm sorry," I whispered into his chest. "I'm sorry. Of course I'll wait for you. I wasn't thinking clearly. That... that Circhos really messed me up."

Charles kissed my forehead, his arms wrapped around me to keep me from leaving prematurely. "You were brilliant, little sister."

Jens cleared his throat to break up our embrace. He was so weird about Charles. Jens snatched up my hand as we walked, and as he stepped out of the forest and across the border of Elvage, we disappeared.

28

COULD HAVE BEEN

lrik was filling out paperwork, which apparently, the elves insisted upon when crossing over into Be. Invisible Charles and Jens went with him, while the rest of us waited in our shared invisibility a safe distance from the portal.

The gold dust in the morning air was mesmerizing, despite the fact that I was still despondent about Thomas Jefferson. The green of Elvage was almost overpowering. While it had rained here, their land was higher above sea level, so nothing flooded too badly.

Jamie and Britta chatted animatedly about the Other Side, and the adventures they were hoping to have there. Foss and I were silent unless pulled, for a moment, into the conversation.

"I want to ride in a car," Jamie admitted. "Jens says they're bigger and faster than horses."

Britta grinned as if Jamie hung the moon. "I want clothes like Lucy's. Just to try," she amended quickly, as if the idea of a woman wearing jeans was a thing that should only be dabbled in. "Do you think they make them for women my size? I'm a far sight taller."

I nodded. "Yup. We'll dress you up however you want to look. Jeans, t-shirt, whatever you like."

Britta wrapped her arm around me, unwilling to let my sour mood rot the grapes of her glee. "Good. Jens always had such amazing stories about your world. It seemed so scary at the time, but now? After all we've seen and been through? I should like to try a new adventure."

"I love you," Jamie said, his fingers entwined through hers. "Can Britta and I get married in your world, *liten syster*?"

I tried to join in their happiness, but I was still pretty down. "Of course. I'm not sure how we'll get you paperwork to be legal citizens. Maybe Jens can figure that out. You can have a wedding and everything. Big white dress, giant cake, the chicken dance – the whole nine yards. Whatever you want, guys."

"I have to talk to you!" Foss blurted out apropos of nothing.

"Who, me?" I touched my chest, unsure of him, as usual.

Foss nodded and stood, walking away from Jamie's side.

"Hey! You can be seen, you know. I can't vanish you if you're not touching me," Jamie reminded us.

"Do you see anyone around?" Foss gestured to the woods that were devoid of people. There were homes in the distance with a handful of bodies moving about, but no one was close to us. We were a safe distance from the portal, and the trees hid us from the four guards quite well.

I stood and followed Foss behind a thick clump of trees so he could say his piece. "I'm warning you, don't push me around today. I'm crabby, and I don't need the stress."

"Clearly." Foss swallowed and fidgeted with the hem of the shirt he'd donned when we reached Elvage. I hadn't seen Foss wear a shirt since we left Fossegrim. When he caught himself doing the nervous action, he crossed his arms over his chest, puffing it out as if to tell me he was in control of the conversation that had yet to happen. "I want you to take me to the Other Side," he commanded.

I looked up at him in disbelief. "You must be joking."

"Don't be difficult."

"What?" My nose scrunched and I took a step back. "Not to be a jerk, but half the reason I'm leaving is to get away from you. You hate me!"

He did not deny this, nor did I expect him to. "I'm a dead man here. I can't go back to my land, and I have nothing. The only property I still own is my ship and you."

I covered my face in my hands, letting out a quiet scream into my palms. "If this is you asking for a favor, you suck at it. No, Foss. Obviously not. You wouldn't last a day on the Other Side. You can't own people over there. You can't hit people. You can't... just everything you do, you can't. Plus, I can't imagine me not strangling you in your sleep if we have to spend another day together."

His eyes showed a hint of insecurity that threatened to tug at my resolve. "You hate me that much? You would send me into hiding for the rest of my days?"

I pursed my lips together and counted to four. "I'm sorry. I'm not being fair. There were lots of things you did that were awesome. Keeping me alive, for one. Every now and then I caught a glimmer of kindness." I ran my hands through my wild hair and then started biting my fingernails. "But Foss? It's not enough. You said it yourself, you like your women silent, and I'm just not that girl. I can't look after you because I can't trust you. You're better off living in the woods. Alrik can help hide you. He's got friends. It won't be a grand life like you had, but it's the most you'll get."

"Please, Lucy. I'm begging, here."

I raised an eyebrow. "Really? This is you begging? Asking almost nicely for once? No."

I turned to leave, but he caught my arm. "I spoke for you in Fossegrim! I gave you my ring to keep you safe. I taught you how to take care of my boat." He lowered his voice as his fingers tightened on my arm. "I held you when you were... and you... in the cabin when I was lost... I don't let anyone care for me, but you did!"

I shook off his grip, trying to maintain my unshaken demeanor. "I did, yes. And you bit my head off the next morning and nearly killed me. I can't live with you, Foss. It hurts too much."

"You kissed me," he countered, a rare glimpse of his vulnerability showing. "I know you care for me. Maybe not in the way you love Jens, but in some way, you do love me."

"And you're a precious little butthole to use that as a bargaining chip to get what you want!" I turned and glared at him. "I kissed you because I didn't want you to be so sad. I wanted to give you something pretty to hold onto so you wouldn't see the world as such a horrible place you had to fight your way through." I rubbed my arms in a self-hug I wished I didn't need. I looked up into his eyes and tried to ignore the insecurity I saw there. "I could have been the friend that calmed you down. I would have taken care of you as long as you needed it, but you shot yourself in the foot. Every time I'm nice to you, you punish me for it. I'm not a masochist, and I won't unleash you on my world. We've got enough problems."

I whirled around to stomp off, only to find Jamie in my path. He'd regarded me with great care since he'd met my brother and witnessed my unraveling. His arm wound around my shoulders as he ushered me forward. "Alrik's coming down the road. We shouldn't be seen." He turned us invisible, and marched us back to Britta where we had front row seats to the undoing of the portal.

29

LOVE THE SWING

When I was a little girl, Uncle Rick used to take Linus and me to the park once a month during his visits so my parents could go out. Not much was memorable about the various playgrounds or beaches he took us to, but the swings always stood in my memory as a shining example of childhood. Linus would busy himself on the slides and such, but I was content on the swings. I recall the feeling of pumping my legs with such vigor, I thought my swing might rocket off the chain. I was also a big fan of Supermaning on my stomach and twisting around so tight, I could feel the chain closing in on my back. Then I'd let myself go, unwinding with speed that made me scream and giggle at the same time.

There was one park, I'm thinking somewhere in Michigan, that was in a beaten-down area. The graffiti on the slide and garbage on the ground did not encourage free play. I ignored the mess and went straight for my favorite thing, my own personal rocket ship on a chain. I pumped my legs all afternoon. When it was time to eat, I begged off the sandwiches as long as I could before Uncle Rick insisted I take a break.

When I pulled my hands away from the chains, the rust clung to my skin, biting into the soft flesh and leaving bloody scratches on my palms. I didn't want to tell my uncle, because I knew he'd make me leave the fun. When I tried to brush the metal flakes and the rust off on my pants, the metal embedded itself more deeply, bringing pain to my attention.

That night had been spent in the ER with a patient doctor carefully tweezing out bits of rust from my hands.

Looking back on it, I realize that's the crux of my problems. I cling too tight, even to the things that hurt me.

Uncle Rick had fed me dozens of Skittles to distract me from the doctor. He'd said, "Goosy, why didn't you let go when you saw the swing was hurting you?"

I'd answered as if the question was a simple one, and not one that would define my dysfunction as an adult. "I didn't let go because I love the swing. I didn't know it would hurt me."

Now, sitting on the hill overlooking my uncle standing in front of the portal, I could not measure the weight bearing down on my shoulders and seeping into my soul. Alrik was going through the semi-private rites of passage with Charles and Jens hidden nearby. While everyone else was watching on pins and needles for the action to start, I struggled to feel anything. I was a person who clung to the things that hurt me. Foss, Uncle Rick, and even Jens could be lumped into that category. I made a promise to myself that I would start over when I got back home. That I would seek out things that added to my life instead of detracted.

Then the action started. Alrik pulled the rake out of thin air (otherwise known as Jens's hands) and whacked the left side of the portal, sending tall bones crumbling to the ground. The guards leaped on my uncle in a hot second, and I could hear Britta's scream that was muffled into her palm.

The struggle was intense. My uncle was older, and the guards were spry. However, I knew better than to underestimate Alrik's ability to pursue to the death the thing he was chasing. He was determined to end Pesta's kingdom, so he did not relinquish the rake even though it was four on one.

I'm not sure what the thought process was in running down the hill to the fray, but when I caught a glimpse of a sword being drawn as my uncle managed to knock down the top of the archway, I found myself barreling toward him, forsaking my invisible compatriots.

"No!" I screamed as I neared them. I could feel my tether to Jamie stretching, and my temples set into their familiar ache.

Out of nowhere, the Mouthpiece appeared. Like, literally out of thin air. I wondered which Tom he had in his pocket. Hulking and angry, he pointed at me and shouted, "Seize the human!"

I ran straight toward my uncle, ignoring the confusion of the guards who were not given to taking orders from anyone, save their elfish rulers.

The guards wrestled my uncle and yanked the rake away from him before the right side of the arch could be destroyed. One of them punched him in the face, and I heard the worst groan from him.

"Stop it! He's an old man!" I cried as I drew several eyes from him with my harried sprinting.

The Mouthpiece ran toward me, not the portal, but his attention was divided when the rake became an object of tug of war. He charged for the rake, and I feared his strength versus Alrik's.

Alrik won the rake and tossed it to me when a guard rammed him from the side. I didn't think; I simply acted. My best swing only knocked down four bones, but we were getting closer to ending it for good. The rake was jerked from me easily, but I avoided a swift punch due to the guard not having been trained to fight someone my size.

In a mess of fighting I couldn't make sense of, Alrik garnered the rake and bashed at the portal's frame again, knocking several of his ancestor's bones to the ground. The light from the portal flickered, but did not fully go out before it was wrestled from him again.

I threw myself into one of the guards, surprisingly

knocking him sideways. As a guard with a red beard stumbled, I sunk my fists into his stomach, though it did little damage other than confuse him. I'm sure I looked haggard from all my weeks on the mission. Plus, I was a short elf to them, which didn't exist. "Move, girl!" Red Beard bellowed, tossing me aside as if I was a fly.

Another guard was thrown off Alrik by my invisible boyfriend, allowing my uncle to struggle free from the other two.

Charles was visible now. He took my lead and punched one of the guards, grabbing the rake that had fallen to the ground in the scrum and tossing it to his uncle.

"He's Huldra! Grab the halfy!" the Mouthpiece accused, fighting his way toward my brother.

"Stop it!" I screamed, lunging for the giant man I kinda knew there was no way I could best.

Red Beard intercepted me, which was probably for the best. I was shoved to the ground and cuffed with some kind of firm cord or rope behind my back. He kept his foot on the small of my back to make sure I didn't annoy him further.

The Mouthpiece let out a barking laugh of victory. "Finally! Tie her up and throw her in the cell!" he commanded. "Pesta requires the human female!"

Even from my spot on the ground, I could tell that the guards didn't take to the Mouthpiece's orders kindly. "This is elfish business. Pesta rules Be, not Elvage," Red Beard reminded him.

Through all the confusion, Alrik managed to break free. I watched in triumph as my uncle raised the rake, slicing it through the air.

But the fated weapon did not hit the remaining bits of the portal. Instead, Alrik swung around and tossed the tool to Charles, who was dumbfounded.

"Finish it!" Alrik commanded his boy.

Then Charles, the Mouthpiece and I watched with open mouths as Uncle Rick stepped through the flickering portal, forfeiting his soul to the land he set out to destroy.

30

CAPTURED

I don't know how long I screamed after I saw Uncle Rick vanish through the portal. I'm not sure I stopped until Charles sprang to action, stunned as he was.

In one fell swoop, my brother bashed the rake through the portal, causing the last of the ancient bones to break and fall. He tossed it in the air, and it turned invisible, thanks to Jens.

Shouts, fists and swords came to fruition before Charles was beside me on the ground getting cuffed. I'm not sure what was the biggest catalyst for my freak-out – losing Uncle Rick to Be or seeing my brother beaten up and cuffed. Whatever the cause, I thrashed around so wildly, the guard had to carry me over his shoulder toward the village. Even then, I did my best to take my anger out on him. I kicked at his head and once even managed to bite his back.

The Mouthpiece got over just enough of his shock at the last portal in Undraland falling to run after me. He grabbed at my ribs, trying to yank me from Red Beard's shoulder. I screamed as his strong fingers bit into me. The two fought over my body, and I fell to the ground with a painful bang to my shoulder.

Four soldiers ran out from the palace and attacked the Mouthpiece, stepping on me in the hub of masculine bodies fighting for dominance.

Pesta screeched out from the Mouthpiece as he was restrained. "Mine! The girl is my prisoner!"

Red Beard was a mixture of confusion and disgust at the Mouthpiece's demands. "You have no rule here, siren! We handle our own criminals!" Cuffs went around the Mouthpiece's hands, but in true Fossegrimen fashion, he broke through the chain.

I screamed as the Mouthpiece lunged for me, his hands around my throat as he jerked me upright. "Finally! You thought you could outsmart me? You thought you could destroy my work and keep your bones?" His breath was hot in my face, but I refused to be intimidated by his dominance. "After all this, I'll relish your screams while I pluck out your bones, one by one." Then in my ear, he whispered, "Your daddy screamed like a dog when I took him apart."

Before I could properly freak out, an arrow flung out from the woods and sunk deep into the burly man's back.

Then another. Then another. Jamie was an amazing shot, and I told him so through the link.

The poor guards were so confused. Two of them ran off into the woods after the invisible source of my favorite marksman. The other two tried to yank out the arrows and revive the Mouthpiece, who was slowly dying a foot away from me.

Red Beard snatched me up and marched toward the palace. I kicked and shouted for him to let me go. Confusion drove my struggle more than anything at that point. *Why the crap would Uncle Rick do that?* I'd seen clearly. He wasn't pushed. He wasn't afraid. He went willingly into the portal, leaving the rest of the dirty work for Charles, who was being dragged behind me, unconscious.

They were not careful with my brother's body, and I was so beside myself with rage, I could not make my words coherent. I wanted them to be gentle with him. He'd just lost his father. Of course, to them, he was responsible for wiping out the retirement and safe haven of every elf alive, so they didn't so much care when he was dragged over rough spots.

My tirade stopped for a brief moment to catch my breath, and I realized my head wasn't hurting from the tether. I tried to look around for Jamie, but my field of vision was limited to the guard's back. I rocked my body as best I could sideways into his head, but he had me pretty firmly locked down. The guards were talking in grave tones to each other about the lasting damage, and beneath my fury, I felt for them. They just wanted a place away from Elvage and the toils of life to retire to, a place to forget their long lives. I understood that.

Images of the Weres flared up in my mind, and I tried to bite the guard's back. For what purpose? I'm not totally sure. I was just pissed, and didn't prefer being carried like a sack of potatoes.

When I paused to figure out the mess I had thrown myself into, I heard Jamie batting against the walls of my brain. *Lucy! Stop it! Just go limp. Say nothing. I'll figure out a way out of this for you two. The less problem you cause, the more chance I'll have.*

What happened with Uncle Rick? Can we get him back? Undo it! That wasn't supposed to happen! And where's Jens?

I tried to ignore the verbal exchanges going on around me so I could hear Jamie. *Jens got stabbed, but Britta and Foss are taking care of him.* Then to quiet my internal and external screaming, he shouted in my head, *He's alright! It wasn't fatal. It just slowed him down, so he wasn't able to stop them from taking you two.*

What do I do? I asked in a pathetic tone. *Why did Uncle Rick go to Be? Was that his plan all along? Or did someone push him in, and I just didn't see it?*

I can't answer that, but from where I stood, it didn't look like an accident. I don't have answers, Lucy, but I need you to keep quiet in there with Mace until I can get you two out.

Okay. I tried once more to kick the guard in the head, but missed.

Lucy! Calm down! Jamie scolded me. *This isn't a slap on the wrist. This is a beheading we're up against.*

That sobered me right quick.

I did not kick or thrash around anymore as the men took us into the castle. Instead of going up to the topmost point, as I had the last time I was here, we went down into the earth. Several stories down, and the panic set in when my head began to hurt again. *Catch up!* I begged Jamie.

I'm trying! I have to talk to the gatekeeper and have him let me through officially. I'm telling them we're laplanded. That should spare your life. They can't be responsible for assassinating a Tomten prince. That would start a war for certain.

Hurry! My head! My temples throbbed, and being hung upside down didn't help matters much. Charles was still unconscious, and I worried about his injuries.

The guards said nothing to us as they untied us, threw us into the metal cage, locked it and left to confer with their superiors up in a room less depressing than this one. Our cell was much bigger than the bird cages they had me locked in on the Isle of Fossegrim, but the psychosis was building up inside me. I fought not to feel Olaf's hand on my body, and choked down the memories that were somehow attached to the Nøkkendalig. The metal box had straw on the floor, making me feel like a cow being herded to its death.

I sucked air through my nostrils, willing my fear not to take over.

Charles. He was still unconscious on the floor. Fabulous distraction.

I got down on my knees and lifted my brother's head off the floor, cradling his shoulders in my lap. His nose was bleeding, so I used his black shirt to stem the flow. I pried open his eyelids, exhaling when his pupils dilated.

"Why?" I asked his sleeping form. "Why did Uncle Rick go through the portal? Did you work out some sort of plan none of us knew about? Why put us through all this just to... Why?" I brushed the black stringy hair away from Mace's face and kissed his forehead. Though he was skinnier and shorter than the other guys, he was still uber tall to me. A solid 6'4", at least. His long legs stretched out on the cold floor, and I longed for a pillow or a blanket or something to help him.

I pushed the jillions of questions I had about Uncle Rick out of my head, lest I go into shock over it all. I hugged Mace to my chest, letting out two large tears – one for confusion, and one for terror. "It's okay, big brother. I'm sure there's a simple explanation for... why he would... He can't be really in Be, can he? Why would he fight so hard against it? Why bring me over here?"

A rat skidded across the floor, and I mashed my lips together through a scream. My fretting inadvertently woke Mace to coherence, and I held him close as he tried to blink his world into focus. "Lucy?"

I don't know why, but I mustered up a tight, cheery smile for him. "I'm here."

"Where? What? Alrik?"

I shook my head. "He's gone. Crossed through the portal and into Be."

Mace covered his beaten face with one hand and let out a mournful cry I knew would haunt me until the end of my days.

31

THE LOVE OF CHARLES MACE

"We've been through this," Mace said bitterly. "He's gone. He left us for Be. What's there to get?"

I folded my arms over my chest at his cross tone, taking up residence on the far side of the eight foot by eight foot prison cell. The air smelled like wet rocks, mold and oxygen that was too thick to move around properly, with none of the suspended gold dust to distract me. "I just don't get it, is all. Why the entire mission? Why put us all through this, just to walk over to the enemy's lair at the last second?"

"He did what he did. He left. Surprised it took him this long. Not exactly a lot to stick around for." He motioned to himself. The chip on his shoulder was so heavy, it physically weighed down his posture.

"It just makes no sense!"

Mace shrugged, the hurt stabbing through his shirt and into his heart, carving out a hole I wasn't sure how to sew back up so he could keep the organ he so desperately needed. "What doesn't make sense? People leave. That's life, Lucy."

"Would you knock it off? That kinda talk isn't helping. I don't know if you noticed, but we're in a prison. Maybe we should focus on getting out of here."

He rolled his eyes, and I could tell he'd been putting on his company manners around me up until this point. Now I was getting a glimpse of Charles behind closed doors. "I'll just whistle us out once they come back down."

"Just like that? You're not worried about the whole off-with-their-heads thing?"

"I really couldn't care less about that right now. The man who raised me just jumped ship on me with no warning. The guillotine would be a welcome distraction at this point."

The heavy door opened, and an elf guard stepped into the room. Charles jumped to his feet and pursed his lips, letting out the beginnings of a whistle.

It wasn't quick enough. The guard shouted in fright, covered his ears, yelled "Huldra!" up the steps and ran back out, slamming the door shut behind him. I made out the words, "This door stays shut until we get the halfy a collar!"

That seemed to snap Charles back into the present. "I can't... it won't work now! They know what I am and what I can do." He shook his head, and then slammed it into the metal bars. "They'll take precautions. They're coming with that noose!" He cried out in agony and clutched his neck, feeling the phantom pains of the collar that had enslaved his gifts and marked him as an outsider. "I can't wear it again, Lucy! I can't! Not after everything we've been through. Not now that I know the power I have." His tail swished around like a panicked dog's, seeking any way out we had not thought of. "Our mom, I can feel her power in me! It's the closest I've ever been to her, and I won't give it up!"

When he started hyperventilating, I ran to stand in front of him, breathing deep so he would remember not to pass out. "Let's not think about that right now." I wrapped him in a hug, rubbing his back and willing him to deflate. "Jamie's nearby. He's trying to reason with the officials to let us go. I'm laplanded to him. That's gotta count for something."

Mace stepped back from me, leaning against the wall and wiping at his eyes. "Jamie's an optimistic fool. His father doesn't care for him anymore than Alrik cared for me. We're a means to an end. There'll be no cavalry coming for him." He sunk to the floor, doom ringing out in his tone. "They won't hesitate to kill us. Even with Jamie attached to you, they'll take action. He's of no value to his kingdom. Everyone knows it. His title means nothing to his father, so it means nothing to the elves."

"Don't say that," I begged. "It's our only hope out of

here." I clicked my fingers. "Wait, porting! Can't you port us out?"

He tapped his shoe to the bar. "Iron. It keeps elves from porting. How else would they be able to hold elfish prisoners?" He looked up at me, pity in his eyes. "Jens would lie to you and be kind, wouldn't he? Sure, Lucy. They'll find a way to break us out, sweet girl. We'll be fugitives, but we'll have our heads."

I glared at his patronizing tone. "Don't talk to me like I'm five. I'm not trying to be naïve. I'm trying to think up something to get us out of here!"

He gave me a sad smile. "To have such optimism. Such hope. Such determination. It must be exhausting, but it's a beautiful thing to watch." Beneath the anger and hurt, I could sense a layer of admiration in the way he looked up at me. "You're always a beautiful thing to watch. I'll take comfort in that as I die."

My nose scrunched and I reared up to attack. "Don't you ever say something so horrible ever again, Charles Mace! We will not die in this cage! We'll figure this out."

"I had a family. For a few months, I had a sister. It was everything I imagined it could be, and more. You were always more. More than you needed to be. More than anyone expected. My life before you was filled with less. To have more? It's the best gift I could've asked for. I love you, Lucy."

Tears welled up in me, and I shouted at him to keep

from feeling his words. "Don't say goodbye! This is stupid! They won't kill me or Jamie or you."

Mace was calm now, resigned to his fate. "They know I destroyed the portal, so my fate's sealed. You would've been saved if you'd stayed hidden."

I bristled. "I would never leave you alone like that. You were in trouble. I don't regret trying to save you for one second."

He smiled a sadness that broke my heart all over again. "I know. It's not in your nature to abandon your family. That's where you're different from our parents. They left me, and then they left you."

I finally sat down, scooting close so I was facing him. I held out my hand and cupped his in an arm-wrestling grip, looking him dead in the eye. "On pain of death, I won't leave you. No matter what, we'll live together on the Other Side, or we'll die together in this cell."

A flicker of something passed through Mace's eyes, and finally, he perked up. "Lucy, I... I might be able to save you and Jamie."

A full beam smile lit my face, chasing away my tears. "I knew you could do it!" I fell forward, embracing him, my chest heaving as the ton of bricks was lifted from it. "When we get to the Other Side, I'm buying you a giant vat of ice cream. Like, with sprinkles and everything."

"Not me," he said, smiling through the pain. "You and Jamie. They saw you trying to attack them, true, but I'm

Huldra. I could confess that I bent your mind to make you do that. I could tell them you had nothing to do with it."

"What?" His words were a sour taste in my mouth. "I would never act like I didn't know you! I can't believe you'd suggest something so disgusting. You're my brother! No, Mace. It's both of us, or none of us." I nodded, pounding my fist to my chest. "To the grave."

"Don't be stubborn. It's the best I can do. There's no sense in you dying down here. You can live, Lucy! Don't die with your pride."

I shook my head. "Don't even try it. I won't leave you. I can't believe you'd even suggest something like that."

Charles drew me to sit next to him, our knees pulled up to our chests as we held hands like children in the dim lantern light. "I've loved every day of being your brother. To know you? It changed me. I always wanted a real family, but to get you? It made all the loneliness of my life before you fade away. I'm so grateful I got to keep you for a time."

I shook my head. "You're doing it again. You're saying goodbye. Knock it off."

"I'm dying soon, Lucy. They don't bother with trials for capitol offenses like this. Now's the time for any goodbye you've got."

I cuddled into his side, the tears flowing as I confronted my mortality yet again. "You know, I've almost died kind of a lot, especially on this trip. Every time I thought I was close, I was okay with it to some extent. I didn't have a whole lot to live for." I squeezed his hand. "But now that we actually might die?" I shook my head, hiccupping through my words. "I want to live!"

It was then I realized the veracity of my words. I was no longer tempted to check out and leave sanity or the world. I wanted to fight, if that's what it took. I wanted to grab onto the people I still had left and never let them go, cherishing them to the hilt. Irony of all ironies to realize all of it on death's door when I had no choice in the matter anymore. I used the back of Mace's hand to wipe my tears away, kissing it twice before I returned it.

Charles was shaking as he put his arm around me. He kissed the top of my head and whispered into my hair. "If that's what you want, then live you shall." He kissed my cheek. "I want you to know that you've been deeply and truly loved. Till my last breath, I'll hold your love in my heart. It'll give me strength and peace as I pass on."

"I won't let you die," I argued. "I love you, Charles. Everything my parents and Alrik did? Messed up. I know your worth. Like stumbling on a treasure chest no one knows is there. You're generous and sincere, and I can't believe anyone ever tried to hold you back. I love you. I love you so much."

"I know." He pulled me closer still, a note of finality dripping over the hug. "I'll hang for this. You won't. And you don't get a choice in this, because you'll make the wrong one."

"Stop talking like that, Charles."

Tears slid down his angular cheeks as emotion rose in

him, puffing up his chest and deflating it as he began to truly cry. "I can make you forget me. I can make it so you won't die for being tied to all this. I'll confess I mind-warped you and Alrik, and they'll be satisfied with my death. They'll turn you free, and you won't have to carry my death around your neck like a talisman." He fingered Linus at my throat.

"What? Obviously not, Charles. That's a terrible plan." I wiped a few of his tears away, but more replaced them. "I would never leave you. We'll go down together." I buried my side into his and leaned my head on his chest.

"You've had too much tragedy around you. I'll be the stranger in the cell with you who gets taken to the slaughter. You'll be the girl with a future, and you'll take it. Go to the Other Side and live. Be with Jens and take your chance at happiness. You'll carry on without the memory of losing yet another family member, and I'll die knowing my sister loves me. I won't see such a beautiful heart so broken." He held my hand to his heart. "I love you, Lucy." He kissed my forehead. "To the death."

Panic built up in me. "Stop talking like that! Think of a new plan!" I flipped through all the possible scenarios in which anything awesome broke us out of this. Out of desperation and complete loss of reality, I leapt to my feet and shook the prison bars, shouting for someone to let us go.

I heard footsteps, weighted and slow, the armor of the elfish guards coming down the stone steps.

Then I heard a whistle. Low and sweet with a note of the saddest tune that simultaneously broke my heart and put it back together. "No!" I screamed, my hands flying to cover my ears.

Mace spun me around and ripped my hands from my ears while I screamed and thrashed in his arms.

"No! Stop it! I won't forget! I won't forget!" I panicked and fought against him with everything I had, but it was ineffectual. "I'll never leave you, Charles!" I struggled to keep my family, but I could feel them all slipping through my fingers. My protests began to melt, and the lucidity of my words started to fog over.

Charles held my arms at my sides, the worst expression of loss washing his face as he whistled his dark melody inches from my besotted expression.

I stopped struggling, my brain feeling oddly confused, like flipping through too many pictures and seeing none of them in the right order.

I felt lips on mine, and like a reflex, I kissed them. The song controlling my heart muffled against my mouth with a strange insistence I could not make sense of.

32

A QUEEN'S PARDON

There was a tall boy crying in front of me, and my heart tugged for his plight. I reached out to him, but he shrunk back from me as the door at the end of the hall burst open and eight hulking elf guards and officials with fur-lined apparatuses covering their ears came marching toward us.

The gate was thrown open, and the emo boy dressed in all black in the cell with me was wrestled to the floor. He thrashed against them with all his might, shouting the most agonized sound I'd ever heard. I couldn't tell if the pain was more physical or emotional, but either way, the trauma was thorough.

I backed up to the wall, trying to make sense of who he was and how I'd gotten into the cell in the first place. My brain worked furiously to put events in order, but they were scrambled. Nothing made sense. I whimpered as they latched a black collar around the guy's neck. He clawed at it, but the lock was firm. The boy barked out a cry of agony, and my heart wrenched for the stranger's plight.

A familiar man clad in all his armor boomed out, "Charles Mace, you've been charged with destroying the portal to the Land of Be, which is property owned by King Hallamar. How do you plead?"

It was Kristoffer. The Head Guard whose pocket I picked when I'd been Queen Lucy in Elvage before. Alrik had needed a key on his ring for... something. Alrik never told me his plans, and now he was in Be. Yet another plan of his I'd been a part of, but been kept in the dark about.

Kristoffer kept his eyes from me and shook the man on the floor. "How do you plead?"

The boy lifted his red face and choked out, "Guilty. I finished my work. I tore down the portal. You all saw me do it."

Without blinking, Kristoffer ruled, "You will be taken to the guillotine." Then he turned to me, hurt and sad as he addressed me, and I felt impossibly small. "Lucy, Queen of the Other Side, you've been charged with aiding Charles Mace in his nefarious quest to destroy the portal to Be. How do you plead?"

I backed up against the cell wall, tears streaming down my face. "I don't know what happened! I don't know how I got here! My uncle went through the portal, but I don't think he was supposed to!" I hugged myself, shrinking into the corner and praying for Jens to save me somehow.

"Please don't put a collar on me! I don't know what I did! If I broke one of your laws, I'm sorry! I'm not from here, so I don't know the rules!" I shrunk to the ground in the corner, hugging my knees to my chest as I cried. "Please don't hurt me!"

They eyed me, suspicious and confused. Kristoffer stared me down, trying to be cold as he calculated my response, but I could see how much he hated that I was in his cell.

The emo guy shook his head, his hands around his collar. "I'm Huldra. The son of Rolf Kincaid and Hilda the Powerful, and you had her banished. I mind-warped Alrik into destroying the portal, but he only did it halfway. Queen Lucy was my backup. She had no idea what she was doing. She met me once, and has been under my control ever since. I stole the key to my old collar. Alrik and Lucy have been mine since then. All of it, my plan."

"Take him to the block!" Kristoffer ruled, helping me off the ground in a manner I deduced to be kind and not a threat. The lanky boy with the black hair gave me an unfathomable look that stayed my heart in my chest before a black hood went over his head and he was dragged off by two of the guards.

"He did what to me?" I asked Kristoffer, who checked my pupils and felt my hands. He stood too close to me, letting me know he was slowly not seeing me as a threat anymore.

His detached expression melted into relief. "Cold! Her

hands are cold and her pupils are dilated. She's been controlled! Kill the halfy now!" he bellowed down the hallway to the two guards, making me jump in my fragile state. Kristoffer wrapped one burly arm around me, rubbing heat into my back to soothe me. "It's alright, your majesty."

"How can he mind-control me? I don't even know him!" I blubbered, burying my face in Kristoffer's armored chest. "What's happening?"

"Queen Lucy, let me take you to the surface. I apologize for your treatment. We had no idea you were being controlled. We had to take precaution, you understand." The apologies came at me from a repentant Kristoffer, but I didn't really process them.

"Jens? Can I see Jens? I don't want to be here! I just want to go home! Can I go back to the Other Side now? I don't know what just happened!"

Kristoffer straightened, donning as much profession-alism as he could while I cried in his arms. "Of course, Queen Lucy. We'll escort you and your Tom straight away. We only request that you forgive us and understand that we were just following procedure. You're welcome to take respite in Elvage as long as you like. Anything you need. We're in your debt."

"Jens! Just take me to Jens," I begged. I had so many questions, but I knew these men were not the ones to ask.

Kristoffer offered his arm to me after bowing his head. "Of course. Right away, your majesty." I leaned on him as his other arm wrapped around me, leading me like a lady instead of the mess that I was. "Elvage begs the forgiveness of you and your people."

"I forgive you. Just let me go home." My legs were heavy as he led me out of the cage and up the few stories that led me to the blinding sun.

33

A PROPER GOODBYE

I bucked backwards when the sunlight hit me. I remember the brightness being too much for me when I first entered Undraland, but somehow I'd adjusted. It seemed my magic had worn off, and now I was trapped by the light.

"I can't see anything!" I informed Kristoffer, who mentioned something about me having some sort of a fit. "Your sun's much brighter than it is in my world. I can't open my eyes! Jamie! Can you take me to Prince Jamie?"

My feet didn't trust me enough to move forward, so they planted themselves at the mouth of the castle. "Milady, Prince Jamie is not far. I can lead you there slowly." Kristoffer's arm around my back moved me down the path, my feet stumbling with nerves and uncertainty. I leaned into his grip while his other armor-coated hand shielded my eyes. Though his hands were rough from work, his caress of my face was gentle.

I heard shouting and knew Jamie was up ahead. He was calling my name and hollering at the guards keeping him on the wrong side of the gate. "Lucy! Lucy, I'm here! Did they hurt you?"

"I'm okay," I called. "Okay" was a broad generalization, but it would do.

Jamie shouted, "I swear on Pesta's broom, if one hair on her head is harmed, Tomten will wage war on Elvage!"

A rustle of armor told me the guards were not pleased with Jamie's mouth. I tried to speed up the pace, but that resulted in me tripping over my own two feet. Kristoffer caught me before I fell to the ground and righted me, apologizing with too much sincerity. His support of me started out more formal, a hand around a proffered arm, but as we walked, that mutated to more of an embrace. He was sweet to me as we walked, considering my delicate state in every step. "It's alright, my queen."

Jamie was let through, and he ran to rescue me from the guard's side. "Lucy! Are you well?" Before I could answer, he barked at the guard in his most royal-sounding cadence, "She could have your head for this! Accusing a queen of such a thing! She's a friend of your court!"

"She was being controlled by Alrik's halfy! How were we supposed to know she was innocent?" Kristoffer explained.

Jamie went silent, but removed me from Kristoffer's

hold and hugged my face to his chest to shield me from the light. I could hear his heartbeat and feel tension in his large hand as it gripped the back of my head. When his voice finally came, it was tight and quiet. "Alrik's ward did this?"

Kristoffer nodded, reaching out in a move uncharacteristic of a guard to stroke my hair. "He was taken to the block and executed privately out of respect for Alrik. Charles Mace admitted to mind-warping Alrik and Queen Lucy the second he was able to get his collar off."

"Charles Mace is dead, then? Good." Jamie swatted Kristoffer's hand from my hair and gripped me tighter to him possessively.

Kristoffer answered, "Yes. His head is being prepared as a gift of apology for Queen Lucy."

"That won't be necessary," Jamie said, speaking for me.

"I insist. We wrongfully imprisoned her because of his actions. She should have confirmation that the source of her discomfort is neutralized." I could tell his face turned toward the castle. "Ah, here comes Boden now with the head."

"Pack that up!" Jamie snarled, his whole body fuming. His grip on my head was painful, and I whimpered into his chest. "She's in a delicate state. You dare hand a woman a severed head?"

Kristoffer backpedaled quickly. "Uh, no. Of course not. A thousand apologies."

"Her Tomten guard requires a healer and a horse, so

we may take her back to the Other Side as quick as possible. Jens the Brave was wounded when he and Queen Lucy fought off and killed the Circhos for you."

Kristoffer gasped and began to ask follow-up questions, but Jamie was on-task. "We'll need paperwork completed and waiting at the gate for the three of us, her Fossegrimen husband, plus her lady's maid."

Kristoffer's head whipped over to me in surprise that I'd married someone from the cursed race. "Yes, your majesty."

Kristoffer left, and Jamie led me out through the gate so slowly, I did not trip once. I clung to him, trying to muscle my way through all the things I wish I had never seen.

"Lucy, I can keep leading you like this, if you wish, or if you'd rather I speed things along, I could…"

I nodded into his chest. "That's fine. Let's get out of here. Fast as we can, Jamie."

In one swift motion, Prince Jamie swept me off my feet and carried me far faster than we had been going. I buried my face in his shoulder, since my eyelids were not a thick enough curtain to shade me from the merciless sun.

When we reached Britta and Foss, who were hiding in the woods far from the portal-turned-crime scene, Jamie let me stand on my own. "Jens is getting stitched up. He'll meet us at the gate."

I looked through his eyes so I could see anything going on around me.

"Where's Mace?" Britta asked, stroking Jamie's muscle as if she was afraid she might have never seen it again. "We should leave as soon as we can."

"How do you know Alrik's ward?" Jamie asked.

"Ward? Uncle Rick had a ward? Like how Robin is Bruce Wayne's ward?" I asked, trying to make sense of anything. How could my uncle have taken in a kid without telling me?

"What?" Britta stepped back. "Is Charles still being held?"

Jamie shook his head. "Charles Mace is dead."

"No!" Britta gasped. Then her voice wavered with tears.

"Did you know him?" Jamie inquired.

Britta cried into her apron. "Why are you asking me that? Of course I knew him! We all know him! Jamie, what's happened to you?"

Jamie was just as confused as I was. "Britta, darling, the boy was executed for tearing down the portal to Elvage. Had we known Alrik had sympathizers to his cause, we could have helped him. He aided our cause, so yes, it is a tragedy."

Foss stood next to Britta, assessing the situation none of us could piece together. "How? How did they kill him, but they let Lucy go?"

The question landed on me, and I shook my face that was covered with my hands. "I don't know what happened! They let me go because he admitted to mind-warping me."

Foss patted my back. "It was good you kept quiet and let them think that. It kept you alive."

"Let them think what? I don't even know the guy! One minute I'm watching Uncle Rick get attacked, I run to help him, he goes through the portal, betraying everything this mission's been about, and that Charles guy picked up the rake and finished the job. I've never seen him in my life before today. Was he a friend of Alrik's?" My tears fell into my palms. "He said he mind-warped me into helping him tear down the portal, so they let me go."

Foss placed his palms atop mine. "They're cold! He did mind-warp her. But why?"

"We should go," Jamie ruled, his hand on my back. "I don't want them changing their minds and deciding we can't cross over. Let's take our chance while we have it."

Jamie picked me up again, but I halted our leave, my voice still shaking. "Wait. This is where we split up. Foss isn't going over with us. Say your goodbyes here, guys."

Jamie put me back down while Britta shook Foss's hand. "Are you certain, Lucy? It doesn't feel right to leave him here. He's got no name, no job, and no money. And Alrik isn't here to help him, either."

As much as it pained me, I was resolute. "I'm sure. He wouldn't last a day on my side. It's not in his nature to be kind. He's Fossegrimen. It's his curse."

It was then that I realized there really was nothing I could have done. I didn't fail in my attempts to turn him into a decent guy. Foss was a cursed man, and there was no undoing that. I began to give myself a little grace for not working a miracle and raising him from the dead.

Jamie and Foss shook hands, saying respectful good-byes in hesitant tones.

My hands over my eyes did not encourage conversation, but that could not be helped. I didn't even know Foss had been staring me down until he growled. "That's it? You're leaving like this? You've got nothing to say to me? How about thanks for keeping you alive? How about thanks for fighting off trolls for you and dealing with everything you handed me?"

"Jeez, Foss! Chill out! I didn't know you were waiting for me to say something. I can't see you, you know. And I've just been through the ringer! I'm stressed enough as it is without your mouth!"

"Could you give us a minute, guys?" he requested, the anger deflating slightly. He waited a few beats and spoke low to me. "Please, Lucy. Please take me with you. I can't start all over with nothing and no one."

I shook my head. "If you want friends, be friendly. If you want money, get a job. I can't be responsible for you over there. You don't respect me enough to listen to me."

"I can learn."

"Don't do this!" I protested, all of a sudden hitting a wall of frustration. My nerves were already frazzled, and my voice took up a higher pitch. "Don't start this all over! I won't ever see you ever again, so don't pick a fight with me as my last memory of you."

"If you want a better one, give me some good news!"

I winced at the brightness when I had only my eyelids to shield me from the sun through the trees. My fingers worked to untie his ring from my neck, but the knot was one of his fancy ones. "Could you help me?"

Foss stepped forward and covered my eyes with his large mitt. "Keep it. It belongs to your dead husband. That man doesn't exist anymore. I have to leave him behind if I'm to start over here."

"But you might need it to trade for food or something."

"I worked too hard for that to trade it for something as common as food." He moved us over to a thicker clump of trees that shaded us from the brunt of the sunlight. It was still too bright for my taste, but I could at least open my eyes a sliver, which I appreciated. Foss sighed, and I could feel his breath on my lips. "Knowing my ring's safe with you? That'll have to be enough to get me through. Will you wear it?" Insecurity in his voice poked through, softening my heart. "For me? For everything we've been through?"

I considered his request, reflecting on the tumultuous ups and downs of our tangled lives. "Okay, Foss. I'll wear it. Thank you." I leaned forward, my cheek landing on his sternum. "When you're terrible, it breaks my heart. I can't handle anymore breaking. Do you understand me? You need me to wear your ring and think about you from time to time? Well, when I do think about you, I need to hope that you're out there making the world better. That you've learned to be kind." I gripped both his biceps and squeezed. "That you're only as strong as you are gentle."

His arms encircled me in a tender hug I wished I didn't draw comfort from. "I can't promise that, Lucy. It's only you that makes me be like this."

I wrapped my arms around his neck, pulling him down so I could hug his cold heart as tight as I wanted. "I do love you, darling husband. And when I think of you, I'll remember the you that lay under the stars on the boat with me, tracing constellations and finding me in the sky."

"I can always find you," he breathed into my ear. A shiver rippled up my spine. "As much as I wish I didn't, I love you. Can't tolerate being around you, but as much as I've ever loved someone, I feel that for you."

"I know." I gulped, nodding into his chest. "And I'll take that with me to my world. It'll make me stronger. It's only a good love if it makes the other person stronger, you know."

"You're plenty strong on your own, lovely wife." Foss found my lips, and we indulged in our last kiss. Emotion swelled up in me like vomit and fireworks – the best and worst of me jumbled up in a ball of nerves and thunder. I wished I could escape him, but part of me knew that as soon as I did, the victory would not be as sweet as I hoped.

It was not a simple token as our other kisses had been, but a complicated mess of lips our fury and angst turned into. Everything with us turned out messy. There was no fiddle music, and Jamie wasn't drunk, but we fell into each other anyway, unable to excuse our desires off as a misstep.

His lips were soft, but the desperation in his kiss was hard and forceful in the way only the best make-out sessions are. He tugged on my hair so my face tilted further up toward him, and I could feel his frustration at his desire for me in every pass of our greedy mouths.

It was greedy, to love two men as I did. It was selfish and childish, and I hated myself for it. That self-hatred made me reckless, so I deepened the kiss, biting his lower lip as his tongue teased mine and scrambled my brains.

Then Foss took control, slowing the kiss to a mournful, languid pace that had more emotion to it than he would ever admit aloud. My heart fluttered and stuttered, and I melted from our attacking kiss into a puddle of delirium in his thick arms.

In his goodbye, I could feel his sadness. It was more than desperation at having to start over; somewhere along the lines of our tangled journey he really had learned to love. It was ugly and turned on a dime, but that was Foss, and I loved him, however overshadowed by Jens that love might be.

He pressed his forehead to mine as we took a moment to catch our breaths. One of his beefy arms was holding me upright as he traced my cheek with his fingers, looking on my face as if I was precious to him and beautiful. As if I mattered beyond the moment.

"Never," he whispered, kissing me in that familiar way couples do when they've had decades of kisses to indulge in. "Never doubt that I loved you."

We pulled away when Jamie *ahem*'d in my head, his unhappiness with my actions reminding me that kissing my husband wouldn't exactly help my relationship with Jens. Foss stroked my lips with his once more as we caught our breath, chuckling at the strangeness that was our hot and cold relationship.

Without asking permission, he picked me up and carried me over to Britta and an impatient Jamie. "I'll carry her to the edge of the woods. She can't be expected to do this blind, and you should get going before Elvage has a chance to change their mind. You can take her the rest of the way."

I could tell Jamie wanted to fight him on this, but didn't really feel like guiding or carrying me the however many miles we still had to go.

I was small in Foss's arms, and for the first time, I truly trusted his strength. It would last probably only until he opened his mouth next, but for that small moment, I was comforted. The confusion surrounding that Mace guy, Uncle Rick and the whole of Undraland faded to the background. It was all kept at bay by my dead husband.

Foss carried me through the forest until the trees became sparse. He kissed my forehead as he let me down, gripping the back of my head like he was afraid to let me go. "Goodbye, lovely wife." He kissed me once more, a closed-mouth blessing I accepted as part of our dysfunction that kept us afloat.

I gave him a sad smile that was probably marred by my

inability to open my eyes. "Have a happy life, darling husband." I held up my fist, and he bumped his to mine, sealing our parting.

He handed me over to Jamie, who took my hand and walked me with Britta to the gate, where Jens was waiting for us. "I don't approve of what you did," Jamie whispered.

"I know. Me neither." I wished I felt nothing for Foss. That my heart only ever wanted what was good for it. That I didn't love the swing that hurt me. If that was so, I wouldn't think twice about flipping Foss the bird and running away. I wouldn't be with Jens, who cheated on me. I wouldn't have followed my uncle on this mission I knew would be too much to handle. If I only did things that were good for me, I would... well, I probably would've died. The Weres, Pesta or just plain life would've taken me down if I didn't allow my plans to get distracted by Jens and his cocky smile that beamed only for me.

Jamie placed my hand in his best friend's, and I felt the rightness in the wrong, the beauty in the black. My life was a mess of madness, but there was one shining point I chose to focus on. I would let him hurt me and heal me, pursue me and be pursued. In my step forward to the Other Side, I realized I was ready to gamble on Jens again.

"I kissed Foss goodbye," I admitted, not willing to go another second holding onto the secret. I felt Jens stiffen, and then try to regain his composure. "It's over," I whispered as he led me to the gatekeeper. "I'm ready to be with just you if you can promise you'll stay with only me this time around."

Jens kissed me, and the guilt of another man's lips on mine in so short a time only sealed my decision.

Jens. Only Jens.

He swallowed. "It's alright you kissed Foss. Thanks for telling me. I did, too, by the way. It's nothing but beg, beg, beg from that guy. 'Jens, I'm in love with you. Toss Lucy aside and run away with me.' It's like every day with that guy. He even got me a bumper sticker that says *Fossegrimens give the best lovin'.*" Jens shrugged. "Finally threw him a bone and kissed him right good."

"You're doing shtick," I observed. "I can tell I really hurt you. I'm sorry. It's just something I had to do to move on."

He kissed my forehead. "I knew you felt something for him. Good for you for finally admitting it."

"Can we leave it in Undraland? I want you. Only you."

"That sounds good." He kissed my lips once, a simple reunion that sealed the deal. "I knew you'd cave. I'm dead sexy."

I grinned against his shoulder. "Take me home, Jens."

He kissed my fingers, and I felt how right we were together. "You got it, Moxie Kincaid. We'll leave Undra in Undraland. Now let's go get you that white picket fence."

Love *Elvage*? Leave a review!

34

THE OTHER SIDE

Enjoy a free preview of *The Other Side*,
Book five in the *Undraland* series:

*E*motions are the strangest things. They hit us in waves, each person experiencing a different decibel of agony or elation, which makes it easy to judge others on their reactions, whether acceptable or not. Uncle Rick crossing over of his own accord into the Land of Be hit us each in varying tones of sadness, denial and confusion.

Britta turned her sadness inward, crying occasionally on our trip over to the Other Side. Jamie swallowed his reaction as best he could, displaying a supportive front to his fiancée, Jens and I. When I tapped into the psychic link we shared, I could feel his emotions swinging like a pendulum from one extreme to the other. I really had no idea how deeply men felt things until getting a peek into Prince Jamie's mind.

After a hushed conversation with his sister as we waited in a small hut that served as the office to the Other Side, Jens was quiet. He made sure our paperwork was filled out correctly, and pushed us through the turnstile with no hint of the personality I loved so much.

After the sucking sensation landed us in the creepy carnival I'd come over to Undraland in, I reached for Jens's hand. He squeezed it for a second, then dropped the connection. Though he'd forgiven me for kissing Foss, I could tell he was still nursing a pretty open wound.

Rickety organ music piped through the park a dismal and irksome tune. Cutouts and murals of terrifying clowns grinned at me, their razor-like teeth sharpened and jagged like broken glass bottles. I dropped my gaze to my toes, only to find their painted faces trying to grab at me and swallow me whole from the floor. The mirrored maze multiplied my heart rate, but when I heard a squeak, I realized it had not come from my mouth.

Britta and Jamie were pressed up against one of the mirrors, aghast at the horror that was the carnival entertainment even I could not muscle through. Jens was so distracted by the emotions he'd stuffed himself to the brim with, that only his sister's yelp and drawn knife brought him somewhat back to the moment.

"Oh, it's okay, Britt. They're fake. They won't bite you." He held my hand and Britta's, nodding Jamie forward. "Almost there, guys."

When the normal noonday sun greeted us, I breathed in the air of a world I had been missing. A hint of pavement, hot dogs, garbage cans, dirt and the rust of machines were all sucked in through my nose, filling me and pushing out the purity of Undra's natural landscape. The rides around me were in various states of disrepair, some missing carts and whole bits of track, but I didn't care.

There was nothing to be done about Uncle Rick, and I'd made my decision about Foss. My family, Nik, Tor and Henry Mancini were enough of a loss to carry. The past would be put behind me, and I would start over. With every step, I began the process of shedding Undraland from my weary bones.

I ran through the amusement park, a burst of energy hitting at the sight of civilization. It was a concrete lamppost that called out to me first. I wrapped my arms around it and kissed the dirty green beauty. "I love you, electricity! I missed you so much!" So grateful was I at being reunited with my world, I did not care about the few carnival attendees who happened to look my way, judging me as a bigger freak show than the one advertised onsite.

Jens watched me with a sad smile. It was as if something big had been at the tip of his tongue since I'd escaped the Elvage prison, but he'd been purposefully keeping his mouth shut. "Cheating on me already, are you?" he questioned, forcing levity into the shtick that just didn't suit. I could tell he was faking humor to attempt a normal disposition, but I thought it was polite not to call him on it. He was hurting.

I kissed the peeling army-colored paint again, running my finger up the slope of the pole. "Only with inanimate objects. Isn't it gorgeous? Look at it, Jens. How many people do you think have kissed this magnificent minx? I might just be the first."

"Lucky lamppost." Again with the impression of a smile.

Britta kept her head down, knowing that she stuck out a little in her Amish-style dress. Jamie's curiosity overpowered his sadness at losing Alrik. His eyes drank in the sights Jens had described to him over the years. His mouth dropped open at the enormity of it all. I checked into our link and smirked at the half-sentences that exploded in his brain in pops and fizzles. *How could that... But the lights with the... The way that moves... I... I...*

I grinned at Jamie, watching the prince come undone at the magnificence of my kingdom. "Pretty great, huh?"

"There aren't words," he mumbled, his mental musings tumbling around his cranium, knocking proper conversation out of his brain.

Jens led us to the ticket booth, where Matilda greeted us warmly. "Hey, Mattie. I need the usual, but for four of us."

Her wrinkled smile faltered when Jens did not offer up a harmless flirt. "What's got you down, James Dean?"

He cast her half a smile, but again, it was hollow. "Alrik crossed over to Be."

Confusion and concern swept over her before she produced an intelligible response. "Be? Are you sure, dear? Alrik? Our man who isn't all that fond of Pesta crossed over to Be? What about his boy?"

Jens was suddenly overcome with a wave of grief. It was fascinating to watch his masculinity suck it down by the gallon until all that was left was a despondent shrug. "Dead. He was a good kid."

I was confused, but waited until Jens finished up with Matilda to inquire about my uncle. "Why does she think Alrik had a son? He was a bachelor, big time." My hand fell into Jens's, but his grip was slack.

Jens swallowed a thick lump before speaking. "Alrik adopted a boy a while back, but he died."

My nose crinkled as I stopped walking. "What? No. He would've mentioned something. I mean, I'm his niece. I think I would know if I had a cousin somewhere, right?" A link clicked in my mind. "Is she talking about Alrik's ward? Charles Mace? Did Alrik adopt Charles Mace? Why wouldn't he tell me something like that?"

Despite the possible onlookers, Jens wrapped me in an unexpected hug, resting his chin atop my head. His heart felt heavy as he leaned some of his burden on me, so I tried to shoulder the weight with grace to let him know I was strong enough for such conversations. "Let's go find a place to sleep, babe. I need to process everything we went through in Undraland. I'll explain everything once I have more answers."

"Okay." Though I had questions aplenty, I leaned up on my toes, cupped his sad face and kissed him. "I just can't believe Uncle Rick would keep something like that from me. I always wanted a cousin. And he's really dead?"

"Please, Loos," Jens begged, and I noticed his eyes moistening. "I can't talk about it yet. Give me some time. We can talk about everything when I figure it out myself."

The sight of Jens in almost tears sent a ripple of shock through me that rocked my worldview. Jens was unshakable. Jens was ninety percent shtick and ten percent mystery. I didn't think there was room in that equation for emotion so thick, it would lead him to tears. I traced under his eyes with my finger, gathering up enough moisture to form one whole tear. "Let's get you somewhere you can rest. Undra was rough on you. I can't imagine how exhausted and sore you must be from all the saving the day you do."

People walking by us either scoffed or pretended not to see us when Jens kissed me. His lips were slow, carrying too much meaning for me to understand. I tried to interpret his affection, but the emotion was heavy, laced with confusing notes that had something to do with Alrik and the secrets my uncle always had up his sleeve. Trust was a funny thing with Uncle Rick. You trusted him with your life, but you knew parts of his truth were lies told right to your face in plain daylight.

Alrik was the only family I had. My sort of uncle and recently adopted kind of dad. Plus, there was the whole strangeness of this deceased mystery cousin.

Jens pulled away and led us to the park's exit. I tried poking around in Jamie's brain for details about Alrik's adopted son.

I don't know, Lucy.

What the crap, Jamie? What gives? Did I really have a cousin? Did I just meet my cousin in that cell minutes before he died?

I don't know. I heard Jamie's mental sigh as we passed through the park's gate. *I just lost Alrik, too. And Foss. And Nik and Tor, for that matter. I need a moment.*

I respected Jamie's space, but the questions kept building inside of me.

Read *The Other Side*,
the next book in the *Undraland* series

ABOUT THE AUTHOR

USA Today bestselling author Mary E. Twomey lives in Michigan with her three adorable children. She enjoys reading, writing, vegetarian cooking, and telling her children fantastic stories about wombats.

While she loves writing fantasy, dystopian, and paranormal tales for her readers, Mary also writes romance under the name Tuesday Embers, and cozy mysteries under the name Molly Maple.

Visit her online at www.maryetwomey.com, and sign up for her newsletter, so you never miss a new release.